Mountain Pony

A STORY OF THE WYOMING ROCKIES

HENRY V. LAROM

Mountain Pony

A STORY OF THE WYOMING ROCKIES

ILLUSTRATED BY ROSS SANTEE

WILDSIDE PRESS

For
C. L. N. L.

Contents

1

The Sorrel That Turned on a Dime

~~~~~~

ANDY MARVIN SLUNG THE MAILBAG ACROSS THE
pommel of his saddle, mounted his little mare, and
trotted down the road from the post office toward his
uncle's ranch. It was a hot summer day with the sun
beating down on the mountain peaks, making the snow
glaciers sparkle. The little mare, called Snippy, shied
delicately at some wandering ranch pigs and kept her
ears busy pointing here and there in search of excitement.

As she left a grove of cottonwoods, her ears jumped
forward, and Snippy stopped so suddenly that Andy
almost slid over her neck. In front of them, a heavy-set
man had just opened a wooden gate and was trying to
lead a bright sorrel horse through it. Andy watched with
interest. An Eastern boy spending his first summer in
the Rockies, he wanted to learn all he could about
handling horses, and this one looked like a bronco.

The man yanked hard on the reins, and the sorrel
pulled back. He jerked again, growling names at the
horse. When the horse reared, Andy noticed that there

was blood on the animal's lips. His eye showed white with fear. He was afraid of the gate and the cattle guard next to it, and he was terrified of the man.

"You loco, jug-headed fool!" the man shouted, and he struck the horse a vicious crack on the side of the jaw with the butt end of a heavy quirt. The horse grunted with pain and reared again, gasping as the man jammed down on the bit.

"Hey, don't do that!" Andy was off his mare before he realized it and running toward the sorrel horse.

The man turned to him slowly. He had a heavy, unshaven face; great muscles rippled under his dirty, blue-denim shirt, and his battered hat showed sweat along the band. "What's it to you?" he asked.

Andy stopped in his tracks. He had no right to tell this grown man, this Westerner, what to do with his horse. "Well, nothing," he said. "Only the pony's scared, and—and his mouth is bleeding."

"Uh-huh." The man looked at Andy coldly. "An' it's my horse, ain't it?"

"Sure," said Andy. "But—but, darn it! That doesn't give you the right to hit him!"

"Why not?" The man hitched his pants and looked down on Andy in disgust. "Look, sonny," he said, "maybe you better get out of the way before you get hurt." He turned and yanked the sorrel's reins again. As the horse reared, terrified of the quirt, his mouth opened, and Andy could see the spade on the bit, a long piece of metal that made the horse gasp and gag,

10

while the side of the bit tore the flesh from the corners of his mouth. Once again the man struck the side of the horse's jaw.

Andy made a jump for his arm. It was like trying to stop a steel piston, but he hung on long enough to break the next blow. Then the man turned, grabbed him by the shirt front, and sent him spinning across the road into the ditch. For a moment he lay there, stunned. Then he felt himself lifted up and pushed backward until he was pinned against a gatepost.

He shook his head to clear it and looked up into the face close to his. He could see the sweat running through the unshaven beard. The eyes, a cold, watery blue, stared into his. "What's your name, sonny?" the man asked, softly.

"Andy Marvin," Andy said, trying to get his breath. He could feel the great fist against his chest, pushing him against the post, grinding it into his back. "Let me go!"

"Wes Marvin's nephew, huh?" the man went on. "I shoulda knowed. You look like him."

Andy began to get his breath back. "You let go of me," he said, "or I'll tell my uncle. He'll pin your ears back."

He felt the fist push him harder into the gatepost. "Let me tell *you* somethin', sonny," the man growled, and his eyes narrowed. "If Wes Marvin starts anythin', I'll tear him apart, see? An' you can tell him Randy Garland said so. An' you! You're a big boy now, sonny.

You got somethin' to learn. Out here a horse is a man's property. If I wanna hit him, I'm agoin' to hit him. Unless you wanna buy him, you got nothin' to say, see? Now git!"

Once again he grabbed Andy's shirt front and, after first drawing him close, pushed him staggering across the road into a pile of rocks.

Andy felt sick at his stomach. He closed his eyes a moment to try and stop the dizziness, and when he opened them again Garland had turned to the horse and was yanking on the bit.

Andy looked at the horse's bright sorrel coat, the silver mane, the broad forehead with the crooked blaze running down the nose. Then he saw the blood on the mouth, the swelling on the side of the jaw. He couldn't stand it any longer.

"All right, I'll buy him," he said.

Garland stopped pulling on the reins and turned in astonishment. "You'll what?"

"I said I'll buy him."

Garland tied the sorrel's reins to the gatepost. His whole attitude seemed to change when he saw the chance to make money. He walked to where Andy was sitting and looked down at him. "How much money you got?" he asked.

Andy was so relieved to see the horse-beating stop that it took him a moment to gather his wits. "I've got some," he ended lamely. Why tell him he had only forty dollars?

Garland scratched his head and made a sucking noise with his teeth. "That horse'll cost you sixty dollars," he said.

Andy's heart sank. He didn't have sixty dollars, and he shouldn't buy a horse anyway. His dad had told him, "Now this money is to make sure you pay your own expenses. Don't waste it!"

And here he was trying to spend it all on a horse, a pony he knew nothing about. A bronc! Maybe a killer!

"Sixty dollars is too much," Andy said.

Garland looked at him shrewdly, a smirk on his lips. "You don't know a good horse from a bad un," he said. "This horse is worth a hundred if I wait an' sell it to the Army feller. I think I'll do that." He turned from Andy and started toward the horse, swinging his quirt.

Andy waited. He remembered stories about how people bargain for horses. Maybe this was a bluff. Garland reached the horse, who immediately began to pull back on the reins. Garland spoke over his shoulder. "You want to make me an offer?"

"Thirty dollars," Andy said.

Garland laughed. "The Army man'll do better."

"The Army won't touch that horse," Andy said bitterly. "You've ruined his mouth. Anyway, I bet he's too small."

Garland turned and studied Andy for a long time. Andy stared back. He began to feel better. The man was uncertain. He wanted that money. And, by golly, the horse *was* too small for the Army. That was a lucky guess.

13

"I'll tell you what I'll do," Garland said, slowly. "I ain't got time to gentle this bronc. I'll give you him for fifty. An' that's my last offer."

"I'll give you forty," said Andy suddenly. "And that's *my* last offer."

"It ain't enough."

"It's all I've got," said Andy honestly. He got up and walked over to where Snippy was cropping the grass. He was doing the bluffing now. He felt Garland's gaze on his back. What if nothing happened? What if Garland just went back to beating the sorrel?

Andy stalled, tightened the girth on his saddle, and reknotted the latigo strap. Trying not to let Garland see the worry on his face, he put his foot in the stirrup and was about to swing into the saddle, when Garland spoke.

"How do I know you even got that much money?"

"Because it's right here in my hip pocket in traveler's checks," said Andy quickly. "I can turn them into cash at the post office any time I want."

Garland sucked on his tooth and scratched himself. "All right," he said finally. "It's a deal. Meet me at the post office in ten minutes." He unhitched the reins and swung into the saddle. The little horse, wild-eyed, its ears back, feeling a cuff on the side of its head, turned on a dime and broke into a dead run, the man slapping its flanks with the quirt.

Andy gazed after them in awe. "Gee," he thought. "That's my horse. *And can he run!*" Then he looked at little Snippy munching grass. "Holy cow, Snip," he said. "What'll Uncle Wes say when he finds out I bought a bronc?"

Returning to the post office, Andy cashed his checks, paid the money into Garland's hands, and in return received a dirty slip of paper stating that he had paid in full for "One sorrel gelding branded R Quarter Box on the right shoulder."

"There's your bronc," said Garland, pointing through a window. "I used your rope and tied him to the hitchin' rack." He folded the money into his pocket and disappeared through the doorway.

To Andy it seemed a simple matter to lead the little sorrel home, but the horse was still frightened. The moment Andy approached, he began to weave and spin at the end of the rope like a trout on a fishline.

Andy unhitched the lead rope from the rail and untied Snippy. Keeping the rope in his right hand, he started to mount the mare. His body, looming suddenly over the mare's back, scared the sorrel, who started backing off. Andy swung into the saddle as quickly as he could, paying out the lead rope as he did so. This seemed to excite Snippy, who began to prance and pivot on her tiny feet. The sorrel, running behind the mare's rump, twisted the rope around Andy's body. Desperately Andy hung on, afraid that, once he let go, the sorrel would get away for good. With both horses twisting and turning, Andy was soon so badly tangled in the lead rope, that there was danger he might suddenly be pulled

With both horses twisting and turning, Andy was soon badly tangled in the lead rope.

from the saddle and dragged. He tried his best to unwind himself by turning Snippy, but the rope cut across his chest and hindered his hands.

In the middle of the excitement, a voice said, "Leave go, cowboy. I'll hold your bronc."

Andy let go the lead rope, turned—and blushed to the roots of his sandy hair. Standing behind him, holding the lead rope in his hand, was Uncle Wes's best friend, Tex Blackwell, the county sheriff.

Wes was the head game warden, and, whenever he and the sheriff met, there were long discussions concerning the condition of elk, bear, deer, and Big Horn sheep. No man in all Wyoming understood animals, wild or tame, better than Tex Blackwell, and there was no one Andy would rather have for a friend.

And now Tex had found Andy all balled up in rope, like a kitten with a ball of yarn. "Gosh, thanks!" Andy murmured, hoping the old man wouldn't laugh at him.

But Tex wasn't looking at Andy; he was watching the sorrel. He shook his head slowly. "You couldn'ta done that, Andy," he said. "Look at that mouth and jaw!"

"Gee, no!" Andy said, hastily. "I didn't do it, sir. I stopped somebody else from doing it."

Tex turned. He had what Andy thought was the most beautiful and luxuriant mustache in all the world, drooping around his mouth, and on his hip he carried a pearl-handled forty-five, the only one Andy had ever seen outside the movies.

"How, Andy?" asked the sheriff. "How'd you stop it?"

"I—I—" Andy felt sillier than ever. "I bought the horse," he blurted.

Tex gazed at him solemnly, with just the faintest twinkle in his eyes. "You got a bronc here," he said. "He's been spoiled. May never be no good. What'd you pay for him?"

"Forty dollars."

"Better give him back, Andy." The old man was trying to be kind. "He's too tough for you, boy. You've only been out here a month or two. Wes'll never let you ride him."

Andy felt a kind of lump in his throat. If Tex said so, it *was* so. He looked at the little horse, his sturdy legs spread wide, his ears cocked forward as if listening to them decide his fate. Give him back to that killer!

"Don't you think I could gentle him, Tex? I mean if I took lots of time?"

Tex smiled. "You sure love horses, don't you, Andy? But you ain't up to handling a bronc yet. You might get hurt bad. You better give him back. I'll fix it for you, an' you won't get in trouble with Wes. Who'd you buy him off?"

"A man named Garland."

The sheriff looked up quickly. "Randy Garland!" He started biting his lip and chewing on his mustache. Andy was surprised. He had never seen Tex show excitement about anything before.

18

"What's the matter, Tex?" he asked. "Have I done something terribly wrong?"

"You better tell me the story, Andy." The sheriff was deadly serious.

Andy's face fell. What had he done? He told the whole story carefully, leaving out nothing.

When he had finished, Tex spoke quietly. "Look, Andy, he said. "When you tell Wes about this, just forget Garland's name, if you can. An' whatever you do, don't tell how you got pushed around. Meantime, I'll see Garland and arrange for him to take the horse back."

"But, Tex—" Andy felt the lump swelling in his throat again.

"I don't like to spoil anybody's fun," Tex said, kindly. "But I'm only savin' you trouble. A Garland horse ain't worth a plug of tobacco in this country, Andy. He spoils 'em. Most of 'em get sold for bear bait. Now here's your lead rope. Take the horse home. I'll see you in the morning."

Once they got started, the sorrel followed Snippy quietly, and for the first time Andy had a chance to think. He felt cornered, desperate. He couldn't bear to give the sorrel back. He had just naturally fallen in love with him. And he was in a worse jam than ever with his Uncle Wes!

He had made enough mistakes with Uncle Wes already, he thought. He had done foolish "dude tricks."

19

like walking his horse through an irrigation dam and flooding the wrong field, and leaving the corral gate unhooked and letting the work horses wander out onto the front lawn.

Now he had spent all his money without permission to bring home a spoiled bronc. He wouldn't be allowed to ride it, and he didn't even have enough cash left to pay for its feed.

And what was all this about Randy Garland? Buying from him was evidently the worst mistake of all.

Andy rode along wondering whether he hadn't better wire his father that he was coming East immediately. "I bet Uncle Wes would be glad to get rid of me," he thought. "He works hard all the time and has enough troubles without me." Well, there was nothing to do but face it. Andy tried to screw up his courage.

But when he got to the ranch all he had to face was a big letdown. Uncle Wes had taken his adopted daughter, Sally, and gone to a game wardens' meeting and would not be back until the following morning. Andy felt tired and discouraged. He ate his supper quickly and said nothing to his Aunt Ida concerning the new horse. She would find out soon enough!

After supper he went down to the corral. The sorrel was tied to the hayrack, eating contentedly. Andy got some salve from the saddle house. Speaking softly, he walked up to the horse and began rubbing his neck. The sorrel tossed his head, but he was over his fright, and Andy finally managed to smear some salve on the sides of the horse's mouth and on the bruised jaw. Then he turned the horse loose in the corral with little Snippy for company.

Andy climbed dejectedly to the top of the fence and sat watching the horses. Snippy munched hay steadily, her head completely out of sight in the rack, but every now and then the sorrel would stop eating and raise his head. His jaws would stop grinding and his ears point forward as though listening to some faint sound far away. Andy wondered if it was the mustang in him, the wild horse listening for a possible enemy.

Once, when he raised his head, a shaft of evening sunlight seemed to pick out the little horse on purpose, and his sorrel coat blazed as bright as a new penny.

"Gee," Andy thought. "If he was really mine! If I could only keep him! I'd call him Sunny."

Dusk rose from the valley like a curtain, crawling up the cliffs. Andy still sat on the fence, dreaming, watching the horse, and thinking, "I'll never get to ride him."

Suddenly he sat up quickly, as though stuck with a pin. "Hey!" he said aloud. "Nobody's told me I couldn't ride him—not yet, anyway." Excitement filled him. "Suppose—suppose I *proved* I could handle him! Suppose I got up early before Uncle Wes got home—"

Andy let out a cowboy yip that echoed up the valley. Sunny pulled his head out of the rack and spun around inquiringly. "You wait!" Andy shook his finger at the horse. "We've got a date at sunrise."

21

2

Battle with a Bronco

~~~~~~

*J*UST BEFORE DAWN THE NEXT MORNING, A COLD BREATH
of wind blew off the snow glaciers and drifted down the
valley of the South Fork. It sent shivers down Andy
Marvin's spine as he closed the kitchen door softly and
started for the saddle house. He dragged his saddle to
the corral, turned Snippy into the cow corral, and closed
the gate behind him. A sorrel head with a crooked little
blaze peered at him from around the corner of the hayrack. Andy started speaking to him quietly. "Nobody's
ever going to hit you again, old boy," he said.

As Andy approached, the sorrel snorted frosty vapor,
then spun swiftly around the corral as close as he could
get to the fence. He trotted high, as though on springs.
He waggled his ears, shook his head, made ruffling noises
with his nose. He felt just fine.

But Andy finally cornered him. He worked slowly.
The horse was head-shy and tried to avoid the hackamore
Andy was attempting to put over his ears so that no bit
would be necessary. It took quite a while but finally it
was on. Then came the blanket and the saddle. He

dropped them on the pony's back gently, talking to him all the time. It seemed to Andy that the saddle didn't fit very well. It humped up on the back. But finally it was tightly cinched and the latigo tied securely.

The time had come! Andy felt a tautness in his stomach. His heart was pounding; his hands felt clammy. This was the moment—the one chance to prove he was man enough to ride his own horse. Sunny seemed to sense the excitement, too. He didn't move as Andy mounted. He just stood hunched a little, his front feet spread wide, his hind legs tucked under him. Andy got well seated, took a grip on the reins, and kicked gently with his heels.

Sunny's head dove between his legs. The legs themselves slammed straight and hard into the ground. Andy felt the horse explode. He thought he had been shot from a cannon. He grasped frantically for the saddle horn, but it was too late. Up, up he sailed. Then he hit the ground with a thudding, stunning bump. Pretty sparklers sputtered before his eyes and from a distance he heard a voice say, "Ride him, cowboy! Ride him!"

When his head cleared, he saw the pony in front of him, snorting with excitement. Leaning on the fence were two laughing men, Sheriff Blackwell and Uncle Wes. Behind them, her feet hanging from a wagon box, sat Sally Marvin.

"Doggone it," Andy grunted, spitting dust and climbing to his feet. He was angry—mad clear through. They were laughing at him and maybe at the horse, too. He

Andy kept on going. Caught by su

ise, he failed to grip with his knees.   —Page 36

Sunny's head dove between his legs.

reached the sorrel, climbed on him as fast as possible, and kicked with his heels again.

As the pony bucked, Andy gripped with his knees. Each jolt shook him, but he hung on grimly, sitting well back in the saddle and keeping his neck stiff. Gradually the jolting ceased, until finally the little horse lined out into a springy trot as easy to ride as a four-door sedan. Andy stayed with it until he was sure that he was in complete control. Then he pulled up in front of the two men.

"I guess Tex told you," he said, looking straight at Uncle Wes. "I—I bought him."

Much to his surprise he saw that Wes was smiling, a bigger, friendlier smile than he had ever seen on his uncle's face before. "Yes," he said, "and—and, by golly, you rode him!"

"You mean," Andy said, "you mean it's all right? I can ride him, and have him and gentle him?"

"You can try," said Uncle Wes.

"And it wouldn't surprise me none if you succeeded," added the sheriff with a grin.

After breakfast, while the women were washing the dishes, the three of them walked back to the corral, and, as ranchers love to do, they sat with their heels hooked on the corral fence and talked "horse." For the first time Andy felt that his uncle really liked him.

"You see, Andy," he was saying, "when you saddle up a horse on a cold morning, he gets a hump in his

27

back that makes the saddle fit badly. The blanket's cold. The cinch is tight. He just naturally wants to get rid of 'em and of you, too. Walk him around a bit first and probably he won't buck a jump."

The sheriff was watching the little horse. "I sure was wrong about that horse," he drawled. "An' about you, too, Andy. You can ride better'n I thought."

Uncle Wes interrupted. "What's that bump on the side of the sorrel's jaw?" he asked. "Looks like he fell on it or something."

Andy answered without thinking. "That's where Randy Garland hit him."

Uncle Wes was rolling a cigarette and had just brought the paper to his lips. He lowered his hands. His thin, sunburned face was suddenly a mask. "Randy Garland," he repeated slowly.

"Now look what you done," the sheriff said to Andy. "Better tell him the whole yarn, I guess."

"Maybe I had," said Andy, shamefacedly.

By the time he got to the part where Garland sent him spinning into the rocks, Wes had turned pale under his tan. The hand that held the half-finished cigarette shook slightly, and the tobacco spilled out little by little on his knee. He threw the paper away and got down slowly from the fence.

"Randy Garland can't push my nephew into a pile of rocks," he said. There was cold anger in his voice. His eyes were steel. "Where is he staying, Tex?" he asked. "I guess I've got to teach him another lesson."

The sheriff clambered off the fence and put a hand on Wes Marvin's shoulder. "Take it easy, Wes," he said. "That's why I come down here. I was afraid you'd get on the prod when you heard about it."

"Why, that game-stealing horse thief, I'll—"

"Now quit it, Wes!" The sheriff's voice was suddenly hard. "Remember Andy interfered with him."

"I don't care. Andy's just a kid. I'm going to—"

"No, you're not!" The sheriff cut him short. "You're goin' to do your best to keep out of his way, Wes. Randy Garland's a free man. He's served his prison sentence. You caught him stealing an' killing game out of season. Now he wants to get *you*, Wes. An' if you pitch into him, I got to arrest you. An' that don't make sense."

At last Andy understood. Uncle Wes loved the game in the hills, the elk, deer, moose, and even the coyotes. That was why he was game warden. He must have caught Garland poaching game and arrested him. That was certainly enough to make a man like Garland hate him.

Uncle Wes and the sheriff stared at each other a long time, the sheriff's arm still on the other man's shoulder. Slowly Wes relaxed; his anger passed.

"All right, old friend," he said. "But some day Randy Garland and I are going to tangle again. I won't touch him now, Tex, but some day we'll have it out."

A few minutes later Andy started his chores. He was responsible for filling the hayracks in the horse and cow corrals, cleaning the cow barn, mowing the tiny

29

lawn in front of the ranch house, filling lamps, and other unskilled, dull jobs.

The truth was that he wasn't much use on a ranch yet, and during the busy summer months Wes had no time to teach him. He had felt out of it, a dude and doomed to remain one, until this morning.

Now, as he struggled with a forkful of hay, he forgot that he was a tenderfoot. He gave no thought to Randy Garland and his uncle's threat. His entire mind was taken up with Sunny and how to train him. He dug into the stack, heaved mightily, and a small chunk not much bigger than the fork itself suddenly came loose and wavered toward the rack.

"If you'd quit standing on the hay you're trying to pitch, it'd come loose easier," a voice said.

Reluctantly, Andy let the thought of Sunny fade from his mind. He heard a laugh and saw Sally Marvin standing below him.

She was slender as an aspen, her face was an even brown, and her blond hair, burned even brighter by the sun, ran wild on her head as though it had never seen a comb. She wore a denim shirt and blue jeans tucked into cowboots.

Andy groaned inwardly. This darn girl knew everything. She could wrangle horses, throw a diamond hitch, ride a buck rake, top a stack—all kinds of things that he couldn't do. She had been away on a visit when he arrived and had returned only a day or two ago. He hadn't seen much of her, but he had heard plenty. She was a top hand, people said.

He shifted his feet off the hay, and a beautiful piece came loose, the biggest he had ever pitched, and went sailing into the rack.

"You see," she said. "It always comes off in layers like that."

"Thanks," he said, blushing and wishing she would go away. He worked loose another layer and tried not to look at her, but from the corner of his eye he could see that she seemed embarrassed, too. She shifted her feet and pushed a wild lock of hair from her forehead. Then irresolutely she started to turn away.

Andy jammed the hayfork into the stack and slid down to the ground. She hadn't paid much attention to him up to now. What did she want? He was curious. "Say," he said. "Thanks for the tip. I guess I could use a lot of 'em."

She looked at him gravely. "I came down here to tell you that—well, that was a darn nice ride you put on this morning."

"Sure," he said. "I've been brushing corral dust off me ever since."

"So what? You got on him again."

"Aw, he didn't buck much the second time." Andy couldn't help feeling pleased.

"No," she said. "He didn't buck hard. But that's not the point. He might have. Anyway, it's like the cowboys say: There's never a horse that couldn't be rode, and never a cowboy that couldn't be throwed."

The conversation stopped. Andy wanted to talk about Sunny, to ask her about training him, but he was afraid she might try to boss him around, to dominate him and the horse, too. That would spoil everything.

Suddenly, she asked, "Can you play baseball? Are you a pitcher?"

"Second base," said Andy, puzzled.

Sally leaned on the fence and rested her chin on a corral pole. "I still throw like a girl," she murmured sadly.

"Well, you *are* a girl," Andy said.

She turned on him angrily. "I know it," she snapped. "And my dad always wished I was a boy. He played shortstop on the Big Horn Basin Bisons for three years."

"Well, maybe you can't throw," said Andy, sympathetically, "but you can do lots of other things like a man. Gee, you can ride and wrangle and rope and darn near everything I wish I could do."

"Look," she said. "I know it makes you feel kind of bad to have a girl around who knows more'n you do about stock. I can't help that. I've lived here ever since my dad died and Wes Marvin adopted me. But I haven't been around with other folks my own age much. There were only four kids at our school last year—three of 'em girls—so I never got to play ball. And I want to. If you'll teach me some baseball, I'll show you everything I can about horses."

"Gee, it's a deal," Andy grinned. "Shake."

As they shook hands, there was a thin call from the house. Aunt Ida, a delicate woman who had to depend rather more than she wished on Sally's help, was calling her daughter.

"Now you see what it's like to be a girl," said Sally resignedly, turning from the fence. "I've got to make the beds, clean the living room, wash the breakfast dishes, and then do a lot of laundry. Don't worry, Andy, you're lucky. Not that I'm complaining. Mother can't do it all and there's no one else, but I'd much rather be a ranch hand."

"Oh, I don't know," Andy smiled ruefully. "This morning I've got to dig myself up to my ears in the compost heap."

But that evening and every evening for weeks afterward they forgot their chores and even baseball to work on Sunny. They rode him out with Sally's horse, Pint, until he was over his fear of gates and fences. They taught him to neck-rein, to break into a dead run in one jump, and to pull up from a gallop at a slight touch of the reins.

Each day he became easier to handle and faster on his feet, but, although Andy was proud of his progress, he knew that at heart Sunny was still a wild-eyed, restless bronc. Whenever Andy mounted, Sunny moved sideways nervously, and his ears were always back listening, not willing to trust the boy in the saddle. Sunny had no love for any man, and Andy knew that sometime, some-where, there would have to be another showdown.

One night, as they were unsaddling, Sally said, "Well, Andy, that's about all I can do for you. What Sunny needs now is a chance to work behind stock."

"You've done plenty," Andy said. "Gee, you've taught me and the horse, too." And never been bossy about it either, he thought.

"I'll tell you what," Sally said, thoughtfully. "Our stock's on the summer range. But we could go up to the Dude Ranch and ask Old Baldy, the corral boss, if you could ride with him. He's got about a hundred and fifty head to wrangle every morning and only one horse wrangler and some dudes."

Old Baldy consented, and one morning at six o'clock, Andy climbed on a horse that felt like caged dynamite. Sunny didn't buck, but he was ready to, and he snorted a menacing cloud of steam into the frosty air as they trotted toward the river.

Sally, slipping out before Aunt Ida was awake, rode little Snippy, who pranced like a dancer, her tiny hoofs hardly touching the ground.

By appointment, they joined the wranglers at the river bar and plunged in, crossing to the horse range, a pile of rough, sage-covered hills pushing up against the sheer mountain peaks. As the ponies splashed across, Andy saw that, besides Baldy, there was a horse wrangler called Jeff and several Dude Ranch guests.

When they entered the range, Baldy pulled up. "Jeff,

you ride upper circle," he said, pointing into the hills, "and take the folks with you. Me and Sally and Andy here'll ride the lower."

As Andy turned to follow Baldy, he saw the sun striking copper from the tips of the western peaks, but down on the range it was still gray dawn. Baldy told them to watch for horses along the skyline or in the hollows where the mountain springs made splashes of vivid green grass below the sagebrush slopes. He pointed out a coyote slinking along the edge of a clump of scrub pine and two antelope watching them curiously from a ridge.

They picked up horses as they went along, adding a few from each gully. Finally, as they topped a butte, Baldy pointed to a mare and colt grazing at the edge of a spring below. "Go get 'em, Andy," he said.

Andy turned Sunny down the side of the butte. This was it, he thought gleefully, real stock work at last. He touched Sunny with his heels, and the little mustang roared into life like a plane on a take-off. Ears back, mane flat in the wind, he ripped down the sidehill, ignoring gopher holes and rocks, turning loose his pent-up energy in a burst of speed.

Andy pulled on the bridle. You weren't supposed to rush down on the stock; you were meant to ease each little group of horses in with the rest of the bunch.

But Sunny disagreed and, grabbing the bit in his teeth, tore down on the two ponies like a rocket gone mad. Andy sawed on the reins, pulled back with all his might, but Sunny kept on running.

The old mare looked up, whinnied loudly to her child, and galloped clumsily away. The colt, squealing with terror, tore after its mother, bucking happily, its stumpy tail bowed over its back like a whisk broom.

Sunny tried to turn and follow them, but his speed was too great. As he hit the edge of the marsh surrounding the spring, he stopped dead in a spray of black mud.

Andy kept on going. Caught by surprise, he failed to grip with his knees. Sailing between Sunny's ears, he spread-eagled into the marsh with a great, squashy thump.

He lay there for a moment, the wind knocked out of him, then he sat up and began rubbing the muck from his eyes. His shirt was black, and he could feel the wet mud seeping through the seat of his pants.

As his vision steadied, he saw Baldy and Sally catch Sunny between them and ride up to the edge of the swamp.

"I guess he doesn't know who's boss yet," Andy sputtered.

"Get back on and show him," Old Baldy said, trying not to laugh.

Sally, Andy noticed angrily, was doubled over her saddle horn, her back heaving. From time to time she peeped over her arm at him, then new gurgles came from her.

Battle with a Bronco

"Gimme my pony," Andy said, furiously. She dropped the reins without looking at him.

Andy climbed on Sunny, his soaking boots making squishy sounds as he slipped them into the stirrups. "O.K.," he said, trying without much success to smile. "Let's go. What are we waiting for?"

Baldy grinned. "Atta boy, Andy," he said quietly. "Stick it out. You'll win that bronc over yet."

By the time they had completed their circle, the sun was beating down on them and the mud on Andy's chest had turned to dust. He brushed it off as best he could, and helped the others to bring the horses down the sidehills.

He handled Sunny gingerly, ready for new tricks, but the little horse seemed satisfied with his triumph. Andy wondered what Sunny would think up next and when the next battle would come.

As they reached the Dude Ranch corrals, Sally said, "Gee, Andy, I'm sorry. I couldn't help but laugh!"

Andy grinned back at her. "Don't blame you," he said ruefully. "Stick around. I think there's some more laughs coming."

They were resting their horses before going home, when they noticed a tired-looking man jogging up to the corrals on a hammer-headed roan. He slipped out of the saddle and started talking to Old Baldy. Soon Jeff, the horse wrangler, and a group of dudes ambled over and joined the conversation, and finally the ranch owner

37

himself appeared, looking neat and fancy in a beaded shirt and frontier pants.

"Something's up," Sally said. "Let's listen in."

She and Andy drifted over to within earshot, and the first thing they heard the owner say was, "I'll give anybody twenty-five dollars if they find the pack horses before tomorrow night."

"Twenty-five dollars!" Sally's eyes grew big.

"Gee, do you think that offer includes us?" Andy asked.

"We can sure find out," Sally said.

3
A Mountain Pony Makes Up His Mind

~~~~~~

THE STORY FLEW LIKE A BRUSH FIRE IN A HIGH WIND. A Dude Ranch pack trip had left about a week before. When they had stopped over in Jackson Hole for some fishing, their pack horses had disappeared. The tired man on the roan horse was Hank Randall, the pack-trip horse wrangler, who had ridden all the way back over the trail hunting for his string. Another trip was due to leave the ranch the following day, and the need for pack ponies was so acute that the Big Boss had offered the reward.

"You let me handle this," Sally said excitedly to Andy. "I'm going to try and dig something out of Old Baldy." The old man, resting easily on his battered kitchen chair tilted against the saddle-house wall, was a fount of cowboy wisdom—if you could get it out of him.

Sally gave him her sweetest smile and poked a gentle finger into his stomach. "Where are they, Baldy?" she asked.

Baldy tilted his hat brim even further over his eyes. "Why, I don't know nothin', Sally," he said. "Mebbe Hank rode plumb through 'em an' thought they was moose."

"Oh, darn you, anyway," Sally laughed. "Look!" she went on, pointing to riders saddling up to hunt the horses. "All these riders are getting a head start on us because you won't tell me anything."

Andy listened and wondered if Baldy, in his own peculiar way, *was* trying to say something.

"Wonder," said Baldy, scratching an ear slowly, "why the supply list of that outfit didn't have any rock salt in it?"

"It didn't?" Sally asked, quickly.

"Nope," Baldy shook his head solemnly, got up and limped into the saddle house, his last two words trailing out behind him. "It didn't."

"I don't get it," Andy said.

Sally didn't answer. She was thinking, scuffling a boot in the dust. Suddenly she came to life. "I do," she said. "Andy, go to the store. Get some crackers, food, anything we can tie on our saddles, while I have a look at a map."

When Andy started toward the store, he noticed several ranch guests who had been watching them, grab their bridles and start for the corrals. "We're going to have company," he thought.

A few minutes later, Andy and Sally jogged up the

road toward the trail for Jackson Hole. "Now maybe you can explain," Andy said. "Where are we going?"

"To Elk Basin," Sally replied. "Baldy hinted that because Hank forgot to take any rock salt for them, the pack horses may have started looking for a salt lick. They would naturally drift back toward home. The map shows that the only near-by salt lick is over to one side of Elk Basin. If Hank came through there at night, he probably missed 'em." She chuckled. "Isn't he a wonderful man, Old Baldy? The last thing he said was, 'If it's too dark to see the brands, you can catch that flea-bitten old Dixie mare. She's got a cinch sore on her belly.' He really thinks we're going to find them, Andy."

They trotted on until they reached the end of the road. Ahead of them, the valley narrowed to a canyon. Jagged peaks cut into the hard, blue sky, snow glaciers sparkled in the sun, and great rockslides, scooped from the mountaintops, lay like poured silver down the sides of the cliffs. It made Andy feel very small, like an ant crawling up a skyscraper.

Just as they entered the trail, Andy looked back. He could see the road winding away down the valley to the distant green of the irrigated ranch fields, and along it the ranch guests galloping their horses.

"Competition!" he pointed.

Sally reined in. "Oh, I wish I had Pint!" she said. "Little Snippy'll never outpace those horses. You lead. I'll do my best to follow."

41

A *Mountain Pony Makes Up His Mind*

When he took the lead, Andy thought, "Those guys know we got something out of Baldy, and they're going to try to cash in on it. But they're not going to get Sally's share, not if I have to outrun 'em all afoot!"

Sunny jogged on up the trail, moving steadily, tirelessly, as though he hadn't already wrangled horses and pitched Andy into a swamp. His feet slammed down on the sharp stone chips as they crossed the rockslides; they scrambled and tore at the roots of trees as he humped his way up the sides of steep creek beds.

Little Snippy tried doggedly to keep up. When Andy glanced behind him, he saw her head weaving as she pushed her shoulders ahead, trying to take long steps. Her ears waggled, as though she had lost interest in sounds and was using every ounce of effort to keep on Sunny's tail.

The trail itself kept moving upward along the river, higher and higher into the mountains. The canyon narrowed until they were riding along the top of sheer cliffs, above a river that tore at the rocks, whirling its way toward the distant plains.

Once they came out on a high rock, covered with moss and a few vividly red Indian paintbrushes. Behind them they could look back for miles to where the valley broadened out into misty hills. They pulled up and watched their back trail. Neither of them spoke. They knew what they were looking for.

Suddenly, at a point where the trail left a grove of aspens, they saw the others, much nearer now, not even

42

a quarter of a mile behind. Andy saw them beating their horses, driving them hard.

"Get going, Andy," Sally said grimly, brushing the hair from her eyes. "They'll be up with us in half an hour easily."

Trying not to look worried, Andy glanced at Snippy. She stood with her head down, breathing hard. She was pretty nearly washed up, Andy thought.

He turned and pushed Sunny along the trail. "How much further?" he called over his shoulder.

"At least three hours," she answered, "if we don't get washed out."

That was the first time Andy noticed the cloud. A great thunderhead swirled around a crater in the mountain ahead of them. Although the rest of the sky was blue, this cloud was full of rain. Andy rubbed his sleeve across his grimy forehead. That was a queer cloud, nasty brownish yellow with bits of scud whirling ahead of it.

"That'll pass over, don't you think?" he yelled.

"Maybe," Sally said. "Only it looks like cloudburst weather."

The trail started down, now, toward the creek bed. Over the rush of the water, Andy heard the grumbling of thunder bounding from one cliff to another, rolling away through distant canyons until it lost itself in some wild and distant land.

As they reached the river bar, Sally yelled, "Pull up, Andy. Snippy's about through." She didn't say anything more, but got off her horse, scooped up some water in

43

her hat brim, and had a long drink. Andy dismounted and splashed his face with the icy water.

"Look," Sally said bitterly, jamming her wet hat over her eyes. "I'm out of it. It just so happens that I was riding Snip instead of Pint. I suppose we might as well give up." She watched Andy for his reaction.

It came quickly. "Can you tell me how to get to this Elk Basin without getting lost?" he asked.

Sally grinned. "You bet I can. It's a tough trail but it's marked with the Shoshone Forest blaze all the way."

"O.K.," said Andy. "You go back. You're the brains of the outfit. You get your share of the money, anyway. Sunny and I'll try to ride 'em off their feet. We'll shake 'em somehow. If I find the ponies, I'll bring 'em in."

"Atta boy, Andy." She slapped him on the back. "I could go further. But Snippy's been a good horse to me since I was a little papoose. I'm not going to kill her off for any amount of money."

"You bet not," said Andy. "She taught me a lot, too."

"There's only one thing." Sally looked up at the boiling clouds ahead. "There's that storm and—"

"Aw, shucks, I've got a slicker. Anyway I don't mind getting wet!"

"No, only—" Sally watched the clouds critically. "That brown scud cloud. That often means cloudbursts. Landslides can be awful dangerous."

"Well, they're just as dangerous here as they are further on. I'll take the chance."

But Sally still hesitated. She started to say something, then stopped, embarrassed.

Suddenly, Andy understood. "I get it," he said. "You're worried about me and Sunny. You're afraid he'll buck me off, or break my leg, or something."

Sally blushed under her tan. "You've got the spunk, Andy," she said. "Only, this is tough country. If something happened—gee, Dad would—"

"That's my lookout," Andy broke in. "I've got to gentle this horse sometime, don't I? And anyway, he's getting tired. He won't start any more mischief today."

"All right," she said finally, "here's what we'll do. You leave me. Beat it on ahead. I'll ride along awhile real easy until they catch up. Then I'll lead 'em up another trail that dead-ends up in some high meadows to the south." She pointed to some high slopes off to the left of the trail. "You keep straight on," she continued, "until you come to where the river forks. Cross it and take the trail up the right fork. It'll take you to Elk Basin. You'll recognize the basin when you get to it. Everything around it's above timber line. Meantime, I think those dudes will follow me. They think Old Baldy gave me some inside dope."

"O.K., pal, and thanks!" Andy mounted quickly. There was no time to lose. Any minute those dudes would come clattering down the sidehill. "Remember, Sally," he said over his shoulder, "I'm riding for you, too."

"Thanks, Andy, and good hunting," she called.

He waved his hand and galloped up the trail. "Maybe they'll follow her for a while," he thought.

There was a flash, a crack of thunder, and rain began to rattle through the branches of the pines. Andy pulled Sunny down to his long, springy trot until he came to a rockslide where millions of small stones had poured down the side of the mountain from the peaks. The trail cut straight across them. Above, all Andy could see was loose rock, below, the roaring river.

The rain beat down so hard that Andy untied the yellow slicker from the back of the saddle. He transferred the food from the slicker to his pockets and the inside of his shirt. Then, while Sunny picked his way across the rocks, Andy started to put the slicker on.

He was just getting his right arm into the stiff oilskin when Sunny stopped, his ears moved back. He suddenly realized that Snippy was no longer behind him. He was alone, and he didn't like it. Furthermore, he didn't like the thunder, the rain, or the waving yellow slicker. He whinnied loudly and spun round in the rocks.

When Andy tried to turn him back and get his arm through the slicker at the same time, Sunny balked. A gust of rain swirled the flapping oilskin against Sunny's flank. He broke into a run, sending hundreds of rocks spinning down into the water below.

For a few seconds, Andy fought grimly with the slicker, then just let it wave. He twisted the reins and tried to turn Sunny up the trail again. Sunny balked and reared. For a moment Andy saw the great piles of rock above him, then the stones gave way beneath Sunny's feet.

Sunny plunged upward, trying to get a foothold in the slithering rocks. He humped and jumped. Andy slammed the reins on his rump and kicked hard with his heels. Below him, Andy heard the water tearing between jagged rocks. He felt the saddle slipping, slipping under him. He kicked with all his might. Sunny gave a final heave, and they hit the firmer footing of the trail again.

But even now Sunny was winning the battle. He was headed down the trail for home. While he got his other arm into his slicker, Andy let him run. But when they were off the rocks and on firmer ground, Andy returned to the fight.

He realized grimly that the time had come to show who was boss, once for all. He had been bucked off once and stampeded once. This time, if he were ever to master the little horse, Andy had to win.

So they fought it out with the rain swirling about them. Sunny banged Andy's leg into a tree, but Andy turned him and tried to make him go up the trail. Sunny turned back, rearing and trying to buck, but Andy kept a tight rein on him, slammed with his heels, and slashed at his rump with the end of the bridle reins.

Then Sunny took another tack. He ran diagonally off the trail and tore under an overhanging branch, trying to loosen Andy from the saddle. Andy was sent over backward. He felt the cantle of the saddle grind into

47

Sunny plunged upward, trying to get a foothold in the slithering rocks.

his back, but he hung on, and once again he turned Sunny back up the trail.

Andy could never remember just how long the battle lasted, but finally Sunny stopped. He was blowing; there was foam on his mouth. He seemed to be trying to decide something. Then he whinnied, loud and long, his whole body shaking with his cry of loneliness. He turned his head around as far as he could toward Andy, as if to say, "Aw, please! Let's call it a day and go home."

"Nope," Andy said aloud, as he touched his heels to Sunny's flanks. "We've still got work to do, Mister."

At last Sunny seemed to make up his mind. He started up the trail and crossed the rockslide. Andy grinned. Sunny had decided who was the boss. Andy had gentled his bronc.

4

Narrow Escape

~~~~~~

*A*S THE THUNDER SLAMMED AROUND THEM AND
the rain poured down, Andy took stock of the situation.
His leg was bruised, there was a large tear in his slicker,
his face was bleeding and scratched from the tree branch,
and the pain in his back where the cantle of his saddle
had dug into him warned him that he was going to be
mighty stiff before he had ridden much farther. A jar
of peanut butter had opened in his shirt, making a
mess before it fell to the ground.

He was sore, bruised, wet, and cold and his hands
were numb, but as he jogged along deeper and deeper
into the mountains, he felt happier than at any time
since he had come West. "This is fun," he thought.
"This is what I came out here for."

Just one thing bothered him. How much time had
he lost fighting Sunny? How long before the others got
wise and followed him?

He rode out of a patch of timber and found himself
at a fork in the trail. The left prong went on, skirting

the edge of the river bar; the right fork, the one he was to follow, crossed the river.

He pulled up a moment under a tall pine. The whole sky was black now. The rain came in gusts. He wondered whether the trail that zigzagged up the mountain on the other side of the river was slippery. Then he examined the trail on his side. It evidently stuck to the river bar for several hundred yards. Here was a chance to confuse the enemy.

Andy rode Sunny up the left fork until the trail was a mass of rocks, and Sunny's footprints were almost immediately blotted out by rain. Then he crossed to the river, entered it and came back until he was opposite the trail again. He crossed, and started up on the other side, hoping that, for a time at least, he had put pursuers off his trail.

His own route went up the side of the mountain in a series of steep switchbacks, and Sunny, scrambling and slithering, had all he could do to keep his feet on the slippery, wet earth. Andy rested him frequently. He had no idea how much farther he had to ride, and even Sunny was showing signs of fatigue.

They had just entered a clump of pines when Sunny stopped and nickered loudly. Andy looked down. He was high on the mountainside now and could watch his trail where it entered the river.

He saw three horsemen, two boys and a girl, pull their horses up at the edge of the stream.

Andy dismounted, pulled Sunny behind a boulder,

51

and tried to put a hand on his nose. He didn't want Sunny to signal his position.

But either the horses below were too tired to be interested, or the roar of the river had smothered the sound of Sunny's whinny. Andy watched the oldest boy, evidently the leader, trying to pick up his trail. He followed it out on the river bar for a hundred feet, then returned to the others, who were standing under the tall pine where Andy had taken shelter a few minutes before.

The two boys and the girl consulted. They were wet through, and their horses, even at this distance, looked tired.

The oldest boy was evidently urging the others to go on. He pointed toward the sidehill where Andy was hiding, as though he had figured out which trail to take. Andy held his breath. This was the moment. He tried furiously to pet Sunny's nose, to keep him from whinnying again.

The rain increased; the wind lashed the trees, and the thunder growled. He saw the girl shake her head vigorously at the leader, then she and the other boy turned down the trail toward the ranch.

But the older boy hesitated. He gazed up at Andy's hiding place, as though unable to make up his mind. Would he decide to keep on by himself? Desperately, Andy tried to keep Sunny from nickering and giving away his position.

Finally, the boy on the river bar turned his horse

slowly and, still looking back as though he were not sure he had made the right decision, followed the others toward home.

Andy waited until they were well out of hearing, and then let loose a damp "yippee" of victory against the mountain walls. Then, climbing stiffly into his damp saddle, he turned Sunny up the trail toward the lowering clouds ahead.

An hour later found him still on the mountainside, skirting the edge of a cliff. In front of him he could see a divide that he thought must lead into Elk Basin.

The rain had stopped. The thunder muttered in the distance, but the clouds still clung to the mountaintops, and Andy wondered how long the dismal gray light would last.

He pushed on steadily. The trail led away from the cliffside and into a clump of pines. Far below him he could hear the river rushing through a canyon. Above him, the mountain, with trees hanging to it, sloped steeply upward. When he came out on a creek bed, cut like a wrinkle down the mountainside, Andy got off for a drink.

He had just dipped his hat into a pool when he heard the thunder. At least that is what it sounded like at first. But it didn't roll away; it grew louder. Andy felt Sunny yank at the reins in his hand. He looked up at a cliff above him, where the creek broke into a little waterfall. To his horror, he saw the white spray disappear. A wall of rolling mud thirty or forty feet high loomed against

53

the sky. Great boulders, plunging toward him, tore out the banks. Trees snapped like matchsticks. The whole great mass was descending on him.

Frozen in terror, Andy looked across at the opposite bank. Too steep. No time to get there.

Involuntarily, Andy had hung on tightly to Sunny's reins. That was what saved his life. Sunny jumped backward, yanking Andy with him. They scrambled back to the edge of the woods, just as the avalanche tore away the entire creek bed behind them. Rocks weighing tons yanked trees larger than telegraph poles out by the roots. The wall of oily mud, ripped from a mountaintop, smashed on down toward the river far below.

Andy leaned, white and shivering, against a near-by tree, Sunny's reins still in his hand. His knees felt weak, as he thought of the difference three or four seconds would have made. He would have been buried, smothered, crushed instantly in that moiling mass. The power of that great wall would pulverize an armored division, flatten a city, obliterate anything in its path. Even here, channeled by the creek bed, it had driven everything within reach to destruction.

Andy watched the creek as it continued to roar past. Not so high as that original terrifying wall, it was still angry, a rolling mass of mud and rock. There was no passing it for many hours. The trail ahead was closed.

Gradually Andy started to regain his nerve. Shakily, he tied Sunny to a tree, took off his saddle, and rubbed him off clumsily with the blanket. Then he sat on the driest spot he could find, got out his soda crackers and chocolate, and tried to pull himself together.

It was really dusk now. As the light faded, the mountains looked bigger—crouching shadows against a lowering sky. Andy was cold, wet, and miserable. His nerves still twitched with fright. For the moment he felt weak and without interest in anything. Lost horses, twenty-five dollars cash, winning a race—what did they matter when you had just been within three seconds of being swept right out of existence.

He choked on a sodden cracker. He wasn't so hungry after all. He just felt small and lonely, a tiny speck of yellow slicker pasted against a wall of heaving mountains.

Andy shivered. "No use losing your nerve," he thought, "after it's all over. You're still alive."

He remembered what his uncle had told him about cloudbursts. The mountains in this section were made of lava and lava ash. When a good big cloudful of rain got caught among the peaks, it was squeezed out in one place like a sponge. The water drained off all at once, tearing bits of mountain along with it, gathering trees, earth, and rocks as it continued the age-old process of erosion.

Andy shook the water from his hat brim, got up, and walked about under the trees, trying to get warm and ease the growing stiffness in his back. "Time to figure stuff out," he thought. "Got to make up my mind. Should I go home now, and start over tomorrow? Or

55

should I stick it out here all night and hit Elk Basin as soon as the creek goes down?"

Andy heard a rustling sound. Sunny was reaching for some leaves on a sapling. He was hungry, too, poor guy! He had eaten nothing since six o'clock that morning. Yes, and he had done all the work!

The thing to do was go home, get a good dinner, give Sunny some of Uncle Wes's precious oats and plenty of hay, and then start out early the next morning.

Then Andy thought of Sally's disappointment and the smile on the faces of the dudes when he returned to the ranch without the horses.

And how about that long dangerous trail over rock-slides and across a river swollen with cloudburst water? There was no moon. He'd have to do most of it afoot, moving slowly from blaze to blaze to keep from getting lost.

"No, by golly!" he said aloud in a thin, damp voice. "I may as well stick it out."

Sunny was well dried off now. Andy tied a saddle rope to the headstall so that the little horse could reach farther for the leaves, took the saddle blanket from his back, picked up the saddle for a pillow and arranged his own soggy bed under the biggest tree. He unfolded the blanket and put it across his chest, wrapped himself tightly in his slicker, and rested his head on his leather cushion.

More than anything he wanted a fire, but a thorough examination of every pocket showed that he had no matches. There was nothing to do but shiver until morning.

As he lay there, trying to find a comfortable position for his aching back, he found himself listening. The water in the creek bed was gradually going down. Near by, he could hear the dripping of the trees. This was a land of mountain lions and bears, he thought. He had heard the men talk of grizzlies prowling into camp at night. He remembered the story of the bear that picked up a camp cook, sleeping bag and all, and ripped him with giant claws. Only the heavy canvas of the bag had saved the man's life.

Andy felt cold sweat on his forehead; a creeping chill crawled up his spine. It was pitch dark now. Every sound—Sunny pawing the ground restlessly, the dripping trees, the slight scratch of a twig—set him shivering again. For the first time, Andy was feeling the loneliness of mountains.

He wished that Sunny had become a pet. Then he wouldn't feel so much alone. Sally's horse, Pint, he thought, would be following Sally around, nuzzling her, asking for sugar. He would have been company. But Sunny! Sunny'd bucked him off, piled him into a swamp, balked, slammed him under a tree. He was still a wild animal at heart, interested only in the friendship of his kind, head-shy, independent, mischievous but—but not a pal.

"Yeah, but the best darn mountain pony in the world," Andy thought loyally.

The night dragged on. In spite of his loneliness and fear, in spite of his sore leg and stiff back, Andy was so tired that he drifted off into a light, troubled sleep.

Suddenly he awoke, screaming. Something cold and wet had bumped his nose. Andy jumped up, tripped over his slicker, and fell headlong. There was a crashing in the brush just behind his head. He yelled again. His heart pounded furiously as he scrambled to his feet.

Then he laughed. Two feet from him, his legs spread wide, his ears cocked forward, was Sunny. He had gradually worked the rope loose, while searching for food, and it was his damp, mushy nose that had bumped into Andy's face.

"By golly!" said Andy. "I believe you're lonesome, too." He limped over and put his arms around Sunny's neck. The little horse didn't move. Andy felt the heat of the pony's body on his arms and chest. He rubbed the neck, enjoying the extra warmth, and it seemed to press down on him. It took him a moment to realize why. Sunny was resting his head on Andy's shoulder and snuffling his nose into the back of his slicker.

Andy felt his loneliness magically disappear. He didn't mind his aching body, his icy feet; he didn't give a hoot for all the grizzly bears in the world. He felt something great and warm and very important—the love between a man and his top saddle horse.

5

Randy Garland, Horse Thief

~~~~~~

*T*HE SUN WAS JUST COMING OVER THE RIM OF ELK
Basin when they reached it the next morning. During the
night the clouds had lifted from the mountaintops, and
the water in the creek had gone down. Andy, shivering
in the icy dawn wind, had led Sunny up the trail to
get warm. At first he was so lame and stiff that he could
barely hobble, but, as the blood began to circulate, he
felt better, and his gnawing hunger almost made him
forget the stabbing pains in his back.

Now, as the sun hit him square on the back, Andy
rolled up his stiff slicker and tied it to the saddle. The
creeping warmth made him sleepy. He wanted to let
himself drift off while Sunny ate his fill of the rich
mountain grass.

Looking down on Elk Basin, he saw that it was about
a mile in circumference, a cup of green grass interspersed
with clumps of pine. Around its edge were stark plateaus,
barren rock with here and there a patch of snow.

But Andy was interested in the parks of green, where
springs evidently sprang from the earth. One of these

must be a salt lick, he thought, and began riding the edge of the basin.

Almost at the same instant that Andy saw a horse's tail flick against a distant grove of timber, Sunny let out a nicker of greeting that nearly shook his ribs apart.

Sunny broke into a trot, and a few minutes later Andy found himself on the edge of a group of horses.

His heart leaped. Here was success—a warm, sunny day, fifteen or more head of horses to drive in for a reward. His mind soared in victory and then dropped like a rock into a canyon.

Something was wrong. The horses didn't look right. Andy rode slowly around the bunch, checking carefully with his memory of what he had been told about the pack string. In the first place, these horses were scrawny and battered-looking, not like the ponies Old Baldy watched over at the ranch. Secondly, not a single one of them carried the Dude Ranch brand on the left shoulder. And, third, there was no flea-bitten gray mare such as Baldy had mentioned, the old pack horse named Dixie with a saddle sore on her belly.

Was there any possibility that he was wrong about it? Andy took his time and tried to wish these horses into the ones he was looking for, but there was no denying it—they were a different bunch.

Andy groaned aloud. All his body aches returned. The sun beat down on him, and he felt so weary that he wanted to drop off his pony and go to sleep where he fell. "No more horse-hunting," he thought. "Even if

60

each one of 'em has a twenty-five-dollar bill glued to his rump."

He slapped himself on the back of the head to wake himself up. He had to figure out what to do next. He was in Elk Basin; he mustn't go to sleep, he mustn't quit until he had ridden around it.

He took his eyes from the offending horses and looked around the horizon. Then he understood. On the other side of the trees, a thin pencil line of smoke rose into a cobalt sky. There was a pack outfit in the basin. This was their string.

"Now suppose," Andy thought, "they are coming over the mountains to the South Fork. Suppose *they* find the pack string! Then they get the twenty-five dollars!"

Andy tried to forget his weariness. He pulled Sunny's reluctant head from the rich grass and began to walk him slowly away from the bunch of ponies. "The thing to do," he thought, "is to ride the basin and see if the Dude Ranch pack string is here. And the less these campers know about me the better."

He rode from one green park to another, winding among trees, along game trails, trying to keep his eyes open.

He might never have seen them if Sunny hadn't whinnied. In spite of himself his eyes had closed; he had been dozing as he rode. Suddenly, he was almost on top of them.

There was no mistake this time. The Dude Ranch

brand was on every shoulder. In the middle of the bunch grazed a flea-bitten gray mare. Just to be sure, Andy dismounted and caught her, felt under her belly, and there, sure enough, was the cinch sore.

Andy breathed a sigh of relief. The warm day, the glaring brightness of the sky, had drained what energy he had. He was too sleepy to be excited again. He sat down under a tree, thinking that a few moments' rest couldn't possibly hurt anything, and Sunny needed grass so badly that he surely wouldn't drift away.

Andy leaned against the tree trunk. "Funny how soft a tree trunk can feel when you're tired," he thought dreamily, slumping further and further down. "Uh-huh —awful nice, though—" He fell into a deep sleep.

"Well, if it ain't Little Joe the Wrangler!"

Andy struggled up through waves of sleep. He knew that voice. He'd heard it before. It was someone he didn't like. He fought his eyes open, and focused them in the bright sun.

Leaning against a tree, picking his teeth with a kitchen match, stood Randy Garland.

Andy rubbed his eyes and started to his feet. What was Garland doing here? Was he after the reward money, too? A sudden jab of pain along his spine made him lean against the tree. Then slowly he straightened up and looked about him.

Behind Garland he saw two riders, one of them—Andy drew his breath in sharply—was leading Sunny.

Randy Garland, Horse Thief

Andy limped out into the sunlight. "Give me my horse, please," he said.

"Just a moment, bub." Garland took the match from his mouth and, stepping in front of Andy, pointed the wet, mashed end of it at Andy's freckled nose. "How in blazes did you get here?"

Andy felt his head throbbing; he was thirsty, hungry, tired, stiff, and had fifteen miles of riding ahead of him. He didn't want to talk to anybody. He just wanted to get going. "I rode up here, naturally, looking for the horses."

"But this bunch belongs to the Dude Ranch. It ain't yours."

"I know that," Andy said. "I came to get 'em. There's a reward out for 'em." He started to brush by Garland to get to the man who held Sunny.

Garland put a big hand on Andy's chest. "Take it easy, bub," he said. He turned and spoke over his shoulder. "Hey, Clint! You and Heinie come here. This kid says there's a re-ward for this bunch."

Evidently Clint was the tall man with a straggling mustache. He walked a heavy-bellied horse over to where they were standing, while Heinie, a fat man wearing dirty suspenders, led Sunny near enough to overhear the conversation. He curled a knee around the saddle horn, took out a plug of tobacco, and slowly bit off a chew. "Re-ward," he bubbled through the tarlike mess. "Why, say, I think maybe we find these horses last night." He grinned broadly. "Yes," he went on with a slight Scandi-

63

navian accent, "I think we seen 'em fifteen, twenty hours ago."

Clint nodded slowly. "Uh-huh. I seen that old flea-bitten mare first thing."

"That's right, bub." Garland pushed Andy gently backward away from Sunny. "You got here too late, see?"

Andy was fully awake now. "No, I don't see," he said. "Anyway, I've got 'em now. And you don't get the reward for just seeing them. You've got to bring 'em in to the Dude Ranch corrals."

"You hear that," Garland said, with mock seriousness to the others. "Somebody's got to haze 'em in, the dude kid says."

"We couldn't let no dude do that," Clint replied. "He might lose 'em."

"Yeah, an' I think I was just going to bring them in anyway," said Heinie, ejecting a stream of tobacco juice.

"Well, I ain't so sure *you* were." Garland took his hand from Andy's chest. "I'm head man around here and I'll decide on that." He walked away from Andy and the three of them, ignoring him as though he didn't exist, began talking in low tones.

So he had done all this work for nothing! He was going to be gypped out of his reward and by, of all people, Uncle Wes's enemy, Randy Garland! Andy straightened his sore shoulders. He'd put up some kind of scrap, but what could he do against three grown men?

For the first time he noticed, in among the Dude

Randy Garland, Horse Thief

Ranch ponies, the horses he had seen earlier in the day, except that this time they were packed. Four or five of them carried camp paraphernalia covered with dirty tarps, the rest simply wore empty pack saddles with the pack ropes wound around the crosstrees. They were a sorry bunch of horses, Andy thought, except for the large gelding the color of coffee and cream. He looked out of place under a pack saddle. "Probably another of Garland's spoiled broncs," Andy thought bitterly.

He tightened his belt and strode out toward the three men. Until he could think of something to do, he might as well hear what they said.

Garland was saying, "You fellers take the packs on out over the platoos an' camp on the Sody Fork. I'll catch you by tomorrow mornin' and split with you."

Andy thought fast. "Maybe you better listen to what I've got to say first," he said. He tried to sound authoritative, but his voice was thin and it cracked a little, which made him angrier than ever.

The three men turned and looked at him in mild surprise, as though he were some strange animal crawling out from under a log.

"Well, now," said the man named Clint, leaning over the pommel of his saddle and staring down at him. "Maybe we should, at that, sonny. What's on your mind?"

"Well, you see, I'm just a dude." Andy tried to look meek. "And I had a kind of wild trip yesterday. Spent

65

the night on the mountain and was almost killed by a cloudburst."

"Well, whaddaya know," said Heinie without interest.

"It was pretty scary," Andy went on, stalling while he thought of what to say next.

"I just bet it was," sneered Garland, shaking his head.

"And that's why they'll have a search party out for me," Andy finished.

He suddenly had the men's attention.

"And that means that Old Baldy and my Uncle Wes and a whole posse of people will be looking for me."

"You don't say," Clint murmured. Both men, a question in their eyes, were looking at Garland now, waiting for him to speak.

Andy squared his shoulders. By golly, they weren't making fun of him now.

Heinie shifted his cud of tobacco and straightened in his saddle. "Aw, let's dangle on, Randy," he said. "I think maybe it ain't worth it. Give the kid his pony, Clint."

But the smell of money, easy money, was still in Garland's nostrils. He waved them back. "Hold up," he said. "How do we know this kid's tellin' the truth?"

Andy played his last card. "Look, Mr. Garland," he said. "My uncle and I always tell the truth. And he said that if he found you interfering with me again, he'd make it hot for you."

Andy's heart sank as he saw the effect of this speech. Garland's eyes narrowed; he made a strange noise in his throat. Turning to his horse, he mounted and, as the others watched, he took Sunny's reins from Clint's hands.

"You two get them packs across the platoos." He spoke tersely. "Keep 'em movin', don't stop for nothin'."

"What are you gonna do?" Clint asked.

"I'm goin' ter see that Wes Marvin don't get no twenty-five dollars from this little squirt."

"Look." Heinie pointed a dirty thumb toward the South Fork trail. "I don't think it so smart to mix with the game warden right now. I think maybe—"

"Shut your face!" Garland spat. "This kid's Wes's nephew. Now get them packs out of here."

Andy didn't understand quite what they were excited about, but there was no doubt who was the boss. The two men turned immediately and started working their pack string away from the Dude Ranch horses, and soon they were lined out across the green park headed away from the South Fork and toward the barren plateau to the west.

Garland watched them critically, still chewing the matchstick and making sucking noises through his teeth. Andy could see he was thinking, planning something. Even though they were strangers, he wished the others hadn't left him alone with Garland. As the pack string disappeared over the rim, the country suddenly seemed bigger, lonelier, with only the two of them. Andy swallowed hard and tried not to show his growing fright.

Garland deliberately dropped Sunny's reins and waved

his arms. "Well, doggone!" he said, showing his yellow teeth. "If that bronc didn't get away from me. Hey, come back here!"

He turned his horse and ran him after Sunny, who, seeing the rider descending on him, snorted, spun, and loped toward his friends in the park. Andy ran into the park crying, "Sunny! Hey, Sunny! Don't go! Come here!"

But Sunny knew when he was being wrangled, and he hated Randy Garland. He kept moving to the far side of the bunch, trailing his reins carefully so that he wouldn't step on them.

Andy stopped running. He clenched his fists in fury. "That was done on purpose," he shouted, as Garland turned his horse and started back toward him. "And you'll pay for this. You'll get it, you—you—" His voice trailed off.

Garland rode up to him and sat there, smiling at him, shaking his head gently. Andy scowled back, taking in the big man and his heavy bay horse with scars around its head. "A scared pony with a broken spirit," Andy thought. The eyes showed white, the ears were back listening for trouble all the time. On the right side of the saddle, under Garland's knee, Andy could see a rifle in its scabbard.

"You shouldn'ta threatened me," said Garland softly. "You're lucky you ain't your uncle. You see, I ain't fig-gerin' on takin' anythin' more from him."

"Mister, you just wait," Andy said.

Randy Garland, Horse Thief

"I ain't goin' to wait." Garland flipped away the soggy matchstick. "I'm awful sorry your pony got away, son. I'm afraid I can't catch him out here in the basin."

"You're sorry! I'll just bet!" Andy said. "What are you going to do?"

"Well," Garland was still smiling. "I'm goin' to take these here ponies, that *I* found last night, down to get the re-ward. When I get to where the trail is narrow, I figger I can catch your pony. I'll tie him to a tree. You can pick him up." He grinned broadly, turned the big horse, and, twirling the end of a saddle rope, started toward the horses.

Andy sat right there in the sun. The thought of walking for miles until he found his horse, supposing that Garland lived up to his word, was too much. He felt sick at his stomach; a wave of dizziness made the trees and the grass and the horses blur in front of him like a badly focused movie. He shut his eyes and pressed his fingers against them. His sore muscles felt heavy on his arms; his back ached dully.

6

The Clue of the Stolen Palomino

~~~~~~

*H*E DIDN'T KNOW HOW LONG HE REMAINED IN THIS position, but when he opened his eyes he was alone. In the distance he could hear Garland whistling at the horses as they headed down the trail for home, but soon that sound, too, was lost and only the raucous cry of a magpie broke the silence of the wilderness.

Andy crawled to a spring that drained into the meadow, where he drank long and deeply. Gratefully, he felt the cool liquid slosh the dust from his throat and creep down to his stomach in a delicious cold line. He took off his hat and buried his whole head in the water and came up snorting, shaking the water from his hair. Then suddenly he paused, listening, his ear close to the ground. Was he hearing things? Was his heart thumping too loud, or were those hoofbeats? Andy brushed the wet hair back from his forehead and a grin broke out between the scratches on his wet face. Horses were coming all right, and fast.

First over the rise, lining out on a dead run, was a dark bay pony with a black mane. On it, riding like a leaf on a fall wind, was a slight figure in blue jeans, with wild blond hair trailing straight out behind.

"Hey, Andy!" Sally called, charging down the hill. "Andy! You all right?" She lifted the reins gently, and Pint sat back on his haunches, spraying dust in front of him.

"You bet I am." Andy forgot his pains. "Have you seen the horses?"

"Sure, and you'll see 'em, too, in a minute. Dad and Old Baldy are bringing them back and Garland with 'em."

As the ponies came over the hill, followed by Uncle Wes on his roan and Baldy riding a black gelding and leading Sunny, Andy laughed aloud. When he saw Garland behind them, his face a mask of anger, he slapped his bruised leg and never noticed it.

"Say, Andy, you all in one piece?" Uncle Wes pulled up his roan and gazed down at him, a worried expression on his face. "Look him over, Sally."

"Aw, I'm all right, Uncle Wes," Andy said. "All I want is my horse back and a chance to put in a claim for the reward on these ponies."

Baldy, a round little lump in the saddle, squinted his pale blue eyes at Andy and presented Sunny's bridle reins. "Here's your bronc," he said, "but about that re-ward, this feller here," he jerked a thumb at Garland, "he's put a claim in, too."

Wes turned to Baldy, and there was just the ghost of a twinkle in his eye as he said, "Well, Baldy, you're

71

corral boss. They're your horses. You've got the authority to decide which of these two cowboys gets the money."

Garland shifted uneasily in his saddle. "Look," he growled. "Never mind the funny stuff. I was bringin' them horses in, an' I've turned 'em over to you. This kid ain't got no claim on 'em."

"Oh, yes, I have," Andy said, rubbing Sunny's neck. "I found these horses first. You were riding by in the other direction, and you know it. All your horses were packed. I mentioned the reward, so you spooked my pony and took the horses away from me."

"Is that so!" Wes turned and looked at Garland, and the fun had gone from his eyes.

"No, it ain't." Garland looked at the ground. "The kid's horse got away from me."

"Phooy!" said Andy. "You spooked him. And you coulda caught him again if you wanted. You've got a rope."

"That's right." Wes's voice was dangerously quiet. "You've got a rope."

Garland's face darkened as the blood crept up under the stubble of beard. He was a man of violent tempers, a dangerous man. With an effort he controlled his voice as he turned to Baldy. "All right," he said. "Make up your mind. Are you going to give me the money or do I have to see your boss?"

"You don't have to see anybody." Baldy's pale eyes showed no emotion whatever. "By the power vested in me as corral boss of the Lazy DR, I hereby give the re-ward for findin' fifteen pack horses to young Andy Marvin, to be presented to him by me as soon as I can squeeze it out of the Old Man."

"Oh, you do, eh?" Garland growled. "We'll see about that. I'm goin' back and put in my claim. This kid didn't do nothin'."

But while he spoke, as though by some prearranged signal, the two men moved up quietly. On his left, Wes Marvin's knee moved against the side of his horse. On his right, he saw Baldy's black sidling up to him.

"You aren't going to do anything but follow your own outfit, Garland," Wes said, levelly.

"Quit crowdin' me." Garland's eyes were deadly.

"If there's any trouble," Wes went on, "I'll have you up for horse stealing—stealing from a boy. Now get going."

Garland glanced from right to left. His horse, feeling the other two closing in on him, began to prance. Suddenly Garland seemed to make up his mind. He jabbed his spurs into the horse's flanks, jumping him forward. As he did so, he reached for his rifle in the scabbard under his knee.

But the gun wasn't there. He spun his horse around, and stared in amazement. Old Baldy, as vacant-eyed as ever, held the gun in one hand by the stock. As Garland's horse leaped forward, Baldy had grabbed the gun and pulled it from the scabbard. "Lose something?" he asked mildly.

"Give me that gun." Garland's anger hit a new pitch.

Baldy gazed at the gun in mild surprise, as though he couldn't understand how it got into his hands. "Come on, give it to me!" Garland moved his horse closer.

"Sure. Just a minute." Baldy backed away, bringing the little carbine into his lap. He examined it curiously, as though he had never seen a gun before, and finally began to work the lever. The cartridges clicked out on the grass until the gun was empty. "Now," Baldy went on, "that's better. The darn thing might go off an' hurt somebody." He held the gun out to Garland, who grabbed it awkwardly and jammed it back in the scabbard.

Wes Marvin, leaning his arms negligently on the pommel of his saddle, waved a finger at him. "Beat it," he said, softly.

"All right." Garland glared at the two of them. "I'll go. But I won't forget this. I was beat out of a fair re-ward, Baldy. But it's Wes Marvin really done it, and some day I'm agoin' to even the score."

"That's right," Wes answered. "There'll be a showdown."

For a moment, Garland and Wes Marvin looked into each other's eyes. Then Garland turned his horse up the trail after his pack outfit.

The others watched him. He didn't look back, but he suddenly jabbed his spurs into the horse's flanks till the horse grunted with pain, slammed his bridle reins across its neck, and disappeared among the trees.

As they listened to the hoofbeats fade into the silence, a magpie squawked in the grove; they could hear the

74

"Now," Baldy went on, "that's better. The darn thing might go off an' hurt somebody." He held the gun out to Garland.

soft tearing sounds as the ponies pulled gently at the grass, and a camp robber flew softly to the ground at their feet, looking for food.

Baldy finally took off his hat and wiped his shiny dome. "Wes," he said, squinting his eyes in the sun, "I think mebbe you're goin' to have trouble with him before snow flies."

Wes took his eyes from the trail thoughtfully. "Uh-huh," he growled. "And you know, Baldy, I rather hope I do!"

But long before the first snow of early fall had powdered the rimrocks they heard of Randy Garland again.

Sally had demanded that their prize money be divided three ways. She took a third, Andy got a third, and Sunny a third—paid off in oats. "After all," Sally said, "Sunny did most of the work!"

Then one night a strange and venerable automobile, steaming in front and rattling behind, clanked into the ranch yard. From it, as though dismounting from a blooded stallion, stepped Sheriff Tex Blackwell, his luxuriant whiskers powdered with dust.

"Hi, cowboy," he yelled cheerfully, as Andy, hazing in the milk cows, rode by on a bareback Sunny. "Light down in the name of the law. You're wanted by the sheriff for questioning."

"Gee!" Andy let the cows find their way to the barn and jumped off his horse. "What have I done, Mr. Blackwell?"

The Clue of the Stolen Palomino

The sheriff grinned broadly and twirled his mustache. "I ain't got a warrant for you, but I'm goin' to ask you a few questions. An' I'm goin' to want some right careful answers."

"You bet, sir." Andy felt a tickle of excitement run up his spine. "What can I tell you?"

"Well, first off, an unofficial question. Is my timin' good? Has your Aunt Ida whanged the supper gong yet?"

Andy laughed. "No, sir," he said. "I'll run and tell her you're here."

When Sally came in from milking, Andy told her about the sheriff's coming questioning. While waiting for supper, Andy thought his curiosity would burst right through the top of his head, but Uncle Wes and the sheriff refused to be hurried. During the meal, they discussed with elaborate unconcern the game situation, then with dessert came the shipping price of cattle, the cost of hay per ton, and, for the benefit of Aunt Ida, all the latest gossip from town. Sally's eyes were big with excitement, and Andy could see the tension building up inside her.

When the interminable meal was over, Wes rolled a cigarette, and the sheriff, filling an old curved-stem pipe, continued to fill Aunt Ida with the doings at last week's church supper. Whatever the reason for the sheriff's sudden appearance, Andy thought, he isn't going to excite Aunt Ida. But this only made him more eager than ever to hear the truth.

At last the sheriff knocked his pipe out in the old sheet-iron stove and said casually, "Say, Andy, how's to go down an' look over that little cayuse of yours?"

"You bet," said Andy jumping up as though shot out of a gun. "Let's go."

The sheriff and Wes strolled toward the corral, with Andy and Sally close on their trail. They leaned on the fence awhile, making comments on the ponies. Finally the sheriff turned and squatted on his haunches, his back against the corral poles.

There was a long silence as the old man filled his pipe again, lit it, and let the blue smoke drift into the still evening air. Now it was coming, Andy thought. This was the moment.

But the sheriff started off casually. "Andy," he said, "I was talkin' about you with Baldy the other day. He says you're goin' to make a top hand."

Andy blushed under his sunburn. When Old Baldy said anything nice about you, even the littlest thing, it was high praise. Baldy wasn't given to compliments.

"He was tellin' me," the sheriff went on, "about your horse hunt up to Elk Basin." He paused, as though considering just how to put the question. Then suddenly he went on. "Now what I want to know is, just how much you remember about horses. You seen Randy Garland's pack string. What can you remember about 'em?"

"Gee, not much!" Andy scratched his head. "They

78

were pretty scrawny. There must have been seventeen or eighteen of them."

"Lot of horses for just three men," said Wes quickly. "Were they all packed?"

"No," Andy said, trying to remember every detail of that morning when he was so sleepy that he could hardly see. "They all had pack saddles, but most of them were empty."

"Uh-huh!" The sheriff nodded his head. "That's kinda natural when you figger on packing a lot of game."

"You mean they were going hunting?" Andy asked. "The season isn't open yet, is it?"

"Nope. Did the other two men with Garland carry rifles?" Wes asked.

"Yes," Andy nodded. "I'm sure they did."

"But," the sheriff went on doggedly, "you don't remember nothin' more about the horses—or mebbe one partickler horse?"

Suddenly, Andy remembered the cream-colored horse with the silver mane. "Yes, by golly, I do!" he said triumphantly. "One of the pack horses was fat and a very light sorrel. Very light—a—a what-you-may-call-'em."

"A palerminer?"

"Yes, I couldn't remember that name—a palomino. And I wondered about him. I couldn't see any brand on him, and, gee, he was a swell-looking horse."

"Good boy," said the sheriff. "Now we have some evidence." He turned to Wes. "Garland's in the Big Game Creek country killin' game like a butcher," he said.

"I don't know why, or just what the idea is, but I know he's doin' it out of season. Mert Simpson, the ranger up there, come down sick yesterday, and he seen 'em. One of 'em was ridin' a palerminer horse. Mert says there was enough shootin' for Army maneuvers." The sheriff paused and his expressionless eyes gazed into the distance. "You gotta go in there, Wes," he said softly. "You've got to get enough evidence to arrest Garland and bring him out."

Andy heard Sally gasp. No wonder they hadn't mentioned anything to Aunt Ida! This was dangerous business.

The sheriff explained that the palomino was stolen from an Easterner who had failed to brand him before turning him out on the range. "But the game's more important," he went on. "Why is he killin' so much? How does he figger on gettin' it out?"

Dusk fell as they talked. Crisp air cut through their denim shirts, and a shiver went up Andy's back which was part cold and part—well, he guessed maybe it was fear at the sound of his uncle's voice.

"Well, I told Garland there was going to be a show-down," drawled Wes, getting up and stretching his legs. "I guess maybe this is it."

Sally's voice came out of the gloom above them where she sat on the fence. "Can you go with him, Tex?"

"Nope, 'fraid not," the sheriff said. "Got a jailful to look after in town."

"Then I'm going with you, Dad," Sally said, jumping

down from the fence. "I'll pack and cook and—well, I can shoot pretty good."

Wes put his arm around his daughter. "I wish you could come, Sally," he said. "But somebody who knows ranch work has to stay here. You know that."

"Well, how about your deputies?" Sally asked.

"Oh, they'll join me in a coupla weeks when the hunting season opens," Wes said. "They've got ranch work to do this time of year. They're shipping this week, you know. Don't worry, honey. I can handle Randy Garland. I've done it before."

The cold night breeze started them for the house. Andy thought of Wes all alone in the hills. He remembered Clint, the shifty-eyed man with the mustache, and Heinie with his sneering, tobacco-stained mouth, and Garland, with the look of hate in his eyes. Uncle Wes had the brains and the courage but, gee, somebody ought to be with him in case something happened. "Uncle Wes," he said, timidly, "I—I won a shooting match at school last year."

"Now there's an idea," said the sheriff. "Take along the boy, here. You can teach him to pack—and he'll be company."

Andy felt his uncle's big, warm hand on his shoulder. "That's a nice thought, kid," he said. "I'll take you in the hills some time. But this business! Well, it's kinda dangerous. Got to send my brother's boy back to school in one piece."

"Aw, gee." Andy suddenly wanted to be with his uncle

81

in the mountains more than anything else in the world. "I—I'd be all right, Uncle Wes. I'd try awful hard to be useful."

"Sure," said the sheriff. "And a feller's got to learn to live in the mountains some time."

"Well—but—" Wes paused. Andy held his breath. Here was adventure hanging on a single word—real adventure, the kind of thing you dream about.

"I think he proved up his claim to a pack trip when he found those ponies for Baldy," the sheriff said, quietly.

Andy wanted to hug the old man. There was silence now. Far away across the range he could hear a coyote yipping his loneliness and inside him he could feel his heart pounding.

"It would be nice," Sally's voice said, "if he could stay in long enough to get his elk."

Andy felt a lump in his throat. Good old Sally! She couldn't go, but she was in there pitching for him.

Wes said finally, "Maybe you're right! And if he's going hunting, Sally, you'd better crawl up in the attic and get him that thirty-thirty. It's a good little gun, and who knows? He might get a chance to use it."

7

Dangerous Duty

〜〜〜〜〜〜〜〜〜〜〜〜〜〜〜〜〜〜〜〜〜〜〜〜〜〜〜〜

*I*T WAS A LIGHT CARBINE. THE SLENDER BARREL GLINTED in the early-morning light; the beautifully machined lever action slid on well-oiled grooves, and when Andy slipped the gun into its scabbard under his stirrup, the smooth feel of the stock caressed his hand.

"O.K., Andy. Turn 'em loose."

Wes, sitting on his strawberry roan, waved toward the pack string. Andy untied the halters, and the pack horses, looking like big white turtles under their tarps, lumbered out of the ranch yard.

Andy mounted and was about to follow when Sally put a hand on Sunny's bridle. "Andy, if anything should happen," she whispered, looking up at him earnestly, "you know, if Dad needs help, get to the ranger station at the foot of the trail and call me on the Forest Service line."

"You bet, Sally. And come and join us if you can, huh?"

"Uh-huh." She stepped back, trying to smile at him as though she didn't mind being left behind.

But Andy thought she looked mighty forlorn, waving to them as they rode through the gate.

A half hour later, with Andy leading and Uncle Wes driving the packs, they toiled up the switchback trail that led to the Big Game Creek country.

Andy couldn't help feeling a sense of importance in riding at the head of the parade, and he thought that Sunny, shaking his golden mane, felt just a bit proud, too. The snug feel of his well-oiled chaps, the professional look of his carefully coiled saddle rope, the glint from the rifle butt plate under his leg, and the thought of unknown adventures behind the mountain peaks, made Andy want to yip and rear Sunny against the sky.

Then, as though answering his feelings, he heard:

"Yip-eee-i-oooooo—eeee
Get along, little dogie.
I know that Wyoming will be your new home."

Turning in his saddle, he saw the usually stern and tired-looking Uncle Wes tossing the end of his saddle rope at the nearest pack horse and bellowing lustily.

So it thrilled him, too, huh! After all *his* years in the mountains!

But old Jug, a Roman-nosed pack horse plodding behind Andy, saw no cause for rejoicing. From time to time he stopped to gaze longingly back toward the ranch, and Andy knew he was dreaming of his old place in the hay corral.

"Phooy on this pack trip!" he snorted plainly.

Behind Jug came Punkin, an aged buckskin and veteran of many trails. He craned his neck for every available shred of grass or even wildflower, tore it gently from the hillside, then munched thoughtfully as he lumbered along.

A black mare called Tarbaby was followed by a big bay known only as "18" from a brand on his flank. This horse, carrying a bright dishpan above his tarp, was something of an outlaw, and Uncle Wes had packed him to break some of his stubbornness before using him as an extra saddle horse.

Finally, wearing no pack and scrambling on and off the trail like a lively puppy, trotted little Snippy, the extra horse for wrangling.

They reached the high shoulder where the trail left the valley of the South Fork and, following the edge of a winding canyon, worked its way toward the distant divide.

But before they could turn the corner, Eighteen stopped. "Phooy on this pack trip!" he snorted plainly. Then, turning directly down the mountain and bunching his legs, he slid toward the valley.

Andy yelled a warning and Wes turned his pony to cut him off. Eighteen slid faster, humping and bumping, starting masses of gravel sliding behind him. The dishpan broke loose and banged in the breeze.

Eighteen bucked, trying to shake off the pan. Then, going crazy from the sound, bucking, crowhopping, half falling, half sliding, he exploded down the hill. As the panniers slammed against his side, the pack rope slipped. Ropes tangled behind his feet. He kicked at them viciously, and Andy saw his duffel bag, extra underwear, socks, and tooth paste go sailing into the sky.

Finally, Eighteen hit the bottom and, with the dishpan clanging like a fire gong, raced for home.

Old Jug and Punkin gazed down sadly at the youngster lining out across the valley with Wes's roan like a bolt of red flame in pursuit, and Andy thought they almost shook their heads in unison, as if to say, "Ah, these youngsters! Won't they ever learn?"

Finally, Andy collected his belongings. Eighteen was caught, repacked, and started on his way, but it was late afternoon when they approached the divide separating the valley of the South Fork from the Big Game Creek country. Above timber line, they crossed the head of a creek, a mere trickle running out from under a ridge of snow glacier.

Suddenly, Andy had an uncontrollable desire to see the other side of the divide. He pushed Sunny ahead, climbed the last switchback, and rode over the top.

To his surprise, instead of walls and peaks, narrow canyons, and snow-capped mountains, a wide valley lay in front of him. A field of purple lupin dropped away to dark stands of pine interspersed with parks of waist-high grass. Mesas stretched into the distance, and far to the north, below a misty ridge, he caught the glint of a lake.

The packs came over the rise, and Uncle Wes pulled

Made of logs with a dirt roof, the cab

oked tiny against the dark forest. —*Page* 93

up his sweat-stained horse, dismounted, and, adjusting a pair of binoculars, examined the country. Andy climbed off Sunny to stretch his cramped legs, but after walking a few steps, he slumped down on a rock, panting heavily.

Uncle Wes lowered the glasses. "Take it easy, kid," he said. "When you're over ten thousand feet, the air's kind of thin. Gets your wind."

Suddenly, the horses' heads snapped up from the lush grass. A shot had echoed up the valley.

Wes spun his glasses toward the sound, and Andy strained his eyes to detect some distant movement, but, except for an eagle gliding in silent circles over the distant lake, nothing stirred.

Uncle Wes slipped his glasses into a saddlebag and started to mount. "Well," he said quietly over his shoulder. "I guess we're in time. The slaughter seems to be on."

The trail descended through woods and fields of wild hay, following a creek that added springs and brooks as it went, growing steadily larger until it became a small river.

Uncle Wes was leading, leaving Andy to wrangle the hungry pack horses. It was almost dark and they were deep in the timber when the pack string stopped, and Andy heard voices ahead of him. He eased by the horses and found Uncle Wes in the middle of the trail facing two horsemen in the dusk.

Andy had never seen either of them before, but, from the lumpy, uneasy way they sat their saddles, he thought they were dudes. The man nearest to him was large and heavy-jowled. Around his neck he wore a loosely tied neckerchief, and hanging from his belt was something rarely seen in the West—an automatic pistol. Both men had rifles in scabbards.

Uncle Wes was saying, "What's your hurry, Mister? Got a bear on your trail?"

The heavy man grunted, "What's it to yer?" It was an Eastern accent, Andy thought, and a tough one.

"Nothing," said Uncle Wes quietly. "Only I heard a shot. Thought maybe it was you. You camping near here?"

"That's right."

"Where?"

The heavy man, shifting in his saddle, brought his automatic slightly forward. "None of yer business," he said. "Scram out of here, will yer, and let me by."

"Sure, in just a minute," Wes said. "I want to know first what you were shooting at just now."

"We didn't shoot at anythin'," the big man said. "Say, who are you anyway?"

"Head game warden. I don't have to tell you that the season isn't open yet."

"Look!" The heavy man moved his horse forward, closer to Wes. "You didn't *see* me shoot anything, did you?"

"No." Wes was watching the man's right hand, the one near the gun. "But you saw me come over the divide, I'll bet."

"O.K.," the man went on. "You didn't see me shoot.

91

You ain't got evidence, and you know where you can go. Now let me by."

"Sure," said Wes, moving his horse slightly. "Just tell anyone you see that the game warden's in, will you?"

The two men, pounding their saddles as they broke into a trot, rode by Andy and disappeared up the trail.

"Ever see 'em before?" Wes asked Andy.

"No, Uncle Wes, and it was too dark to recognize the horses."

Wes tipped his Stetson over his eyes and scratched the back of his head. "Funny!" he said. "If they're Garland's dudes, I can't see where he got 'em from."

"Down in Jackson Hole, maybe," Andy said.

"I called the Hole last night. Garland never showed up there. Sure strange!"

They rode on through the twilight, and a few minutes later old Punkin, forever in search of food, strayed from the trail. Andy was trotting after him, when Sunny jumped sideways so fast that he almost threw Andy from the saddle. Andy grabbed the horn and kicked Sunny ahead, but the little horse backed away, snorting with fright.

Then Andy saw the body lying in the tall grass. He dismounted and walked cautiously up to it.

A young deer, a doe, her body still warm, lay just where she had fallen, a bullet through her shoulder. Andy leaned down to examine her closely in the fading light. His throat tightened. Although lying on her side, her slender little legs and tiny hoofs were still bunched as though she were running. And her eyes, large and brown, carried a hurt expression, a look of surprise and reproach.

Almost human, Andy thought, biting his lip. He got up and turned away, beating back a burning sensation behind his eyes.

"It's murder," he mumbled aloud. "Just murder."

"You bet it is, Andy." He looked up and saw Wes watching him from his horse. "It's not murder if you need the meat. But these fellers just kill for fun. And they sure shoot better than they ride."

Andy felt the anger rising in him. "Let's go get 'em, Uncle Wes," he said. "Get 'em now!"

Wes smiled down at him. "Don't worry, kid," he said. "That's what we're up here for. But let's get 'em *all*—including Randy Garland."

The moon was high over the pines when they reached their camp, a trapper's cabin near Big Game Creek. Made of logs with a dirt roof, it looked tiny against the dark forest. To one side, Andy saw a neat pole corral, and in front of it a meadow of such wonderful grass that even old Punkin would be satisfied. They tied the pack horses to trees, unpacked, and covered each saddle and blanket with tarps against the dew.

While Uncle Wes drove a stake with the ax and picketed little Snippy in the meadow, the other ponies found a dusty spot and rolled their sweaty backs in it, grunting and snorting with delight.

Old Jug, the horse most likely to wander, was fitted

with a large cowbell that rang with a mellow tone as the ponies started grazing. And only Snippy, fearful of being left behind, whinnied into the night until the echoes bounced back from a distant ridge.

Uncle Wes lighted a lantern and they entered the cabin. The first thing Andy noticed was an open sack with flour running out on the dirt floor. Half-empty cans of coffee and sugar, dirty dishes, a filthy frying pan, burned matches, and cigarette butts were strewn about, turning the little room into a shambles.

Uncle Wes leaned against the doorway and stared at the mess inside. Andy could hear him breathing deeply and knew that his uncle was too angry to speak. Finally, still without a word, he went to work, and not until the cabin was thoroughly cleaned and swept did he turn and shake a finger at Andy.

"It used to be in the mountain country that every man left his door open so a stranger could use his cabin," he growled. "When a man ran short of flour or something, he helped himself and left something else in exchange. But he always left the cabin neat and clean like he found it." He threw the broom into a corner furiously. "The only worry was pack rats," he grunted. "Now it's the *human* kind! Those fellers we met on the trail—they did this."

He looked at Andy, and at last his eyes softened into a smile. "Great snakes, you must be starving," he said. "Go wash this skillet and we'll eat."

After Uncle Wes had filled Andy with fried ham,

94

beans, fluffy sourdough biscuits topped off with a can of apricots, they laid their bedrolls out under the stars. Andy was dead tired after thirty-odd miles of riding, but when he closed his eyes, he saw again the body lying in the grass, the great haunting eyes filled with reproach. Was there a little fawn out there now, alone, deserted, looking for its mother?

Andy stirred restlessly. He heard Snippy cropping grass near by and the faint sound of Jug's bell in the distance told him where the other horses were grazing.

"What's the matter, kid?" Uncle Wes's voice came out of the dark.

"It's that doe we saw," Andy answered. "Do you suppose she's got a fawn, maybe?"

"Maybe." Wes's voice was warm. "But don't worry, old man. The little feller's old enough to take care of himself by now."

Andy felt better and was just dropping off when Wes shouted, "Andy, watch it!"

Andy sat up. Over him loomed a shadow, cutting off the waning moonlight. It looked enormous from the ground, towering over him. Then it made a slight snuffling noise.

"Oh, gee!" Andy was embarrassed. "It's Sunny!"

"Well, of all the darn fool horses!" Uncle Wes chuckled. "What's he leave the bunch and come back here for?"

"Well," Andy blushed in the dark, "at the ranch—

that is, I guess it's the time I usually sneak him a carrot."

"Oh, so you sneak my carrots, do you? Then how are you going to fix him up now?"

Andy wondered if Uncle Wes would be angry. "I've —I've got a few in my duffel bag."

Uncle Wes laughed aloud. "Well, for the love o' Mike get 'em and feed him before he tromps us both to death."

8

The Mystery of the Game Rustlers

~~~~~~~~~~~~~~~~~~~~~~~~~~~~~~~~~~

B Y THE TIME ANDY AWOKE THE NEXT MORNING, THE sun was poking a golden shaft through the pines, and Uncle Wes, on Snippy, was hazing the horses across the meadow into camp.

After a breakfast of bacon, eggs, and hotcakes, Uncle Wes led Eighteen from the corral. "My old roan's kind of leg-weary," he said. "I think it's time to top off old toughie, here."

Andy had never seen his uncle ride a bronc. Wes slipped on a hackamore and followed with the blanket and saddle, petting the horse's neck from time to time and talking to it quietly. When everything was ready and the cinch tested carefully, Wes took off his own wide leather belt and doubled it carefully in his right hand.

"Stand back, Andy," he said as he slipped into the saddle. "Old Eighteen's got a hump in his back." He touched his spurs, still petting the horse's neck and talking to it.

Eighteen reared, plunged his head, and came down

stiff-legged. Andy felt the ground tremble as the horse pounded the turf, twisting like a snake.

Each time the horse bucked, Uncle Wes, deep in the saddle, slapped its rump with the belt. It stung without bruising, but it cracked like a pistol shot. Eighteen snorted, grunted, waved his head. He sunfished, crow-hopped, but most of all he pounded the ground in hard-driving bucks, trying to shake Wes off.

But Wes just didn't come loose. Finally, Eighteen's head came up. Immediately, Wes stopped hitting him with the harmless belt. Eighteen made one more half-hearted jump, then broke into a gallop and disappeared across the meadow.

A few minutes later, Andy saw them returning, Eighteen trotting easily with Uncle Wes patting his neck and talking to him. "I guess we can go now," he yelled at Andy. "This old outlaw tells me he's through for the day."

Andy mounted Sunny. "Oh, brother," he thought, admiration in his eyes. "Can my uncle ever ride!"

As they rode up the trail of the night before, Uncle Wes watched the ground carefully. "First we'll track these dudes back to their camp," he said.

"You mean you're going to walk right in on 'em?" Andy asked, thinking of the automatic the heavy man had worn.

"Sure," Wes answered. "And if we find any meat— we've got 'em!" He pulled up suddenly and pointed to the right. "I thought so," he said. "They're in Lost Basin."

"Where's that?" Andy asked.

"It wouldn't hurt any to show you," Wes said, dismounting. "You might need to find your way by yourself sometime." He cut a willow stick, squatted on his heels, and drew a rough circle in the dust of the trail. "You see," he said, "this country's kind of like a blue-plate special at the Elkhorn Restaurant. You know, one of those plates with divisions in it for meat and vegetables. It's a flat country surrounded by mountains with ridges and mesas running across it. Now here we are in the meat part of the plate." He scratched with the stick. "If we kept riding down Big Game Creek we'd hit a ridge and sooner or later we'd be in the potato section. But if we turn west here and climb the ridge into Lost Basin, that'll land us with the vegetables." He stood up and grinned at Andy. "And I've got a hunch," he concluded, "we're going to find Randy Garland somewhere in the succotash."

The trail up the ridge to Lost Basin was badly marked and very steep. Little Sunny scrambled up it with ease, but Eighteen, who was far from bridle-wise, balked from time to time, and Wes was forced to pull his head around, teaching him as they rode.

They were almost at the top of the ridge when Andy heard hoofbeats in front of them. They were sudden, as though someone had been startled into gallop.

99

Wes pulled up and turned in the saddle. "They're expecting us," he said dryly. "They put out sentries."

Andy wanted to top the ridge and get a view of Lost Basin, but Wes decided to leave the trail and work along behind the rim. "There's no use showing up just where you're expected," he said. "And, anyway, let's have a look at 'em first."

They wove their horses among the trees, slithered down dry gulches, and scrambled up banks among the aspens until they had ridden another mile. Then, when they reached a dense grove of pines, they dismounted, tied their horses, and walked to the top of the ridge. There, resting on the very peak, stood a large rock, poised so that Andy thought a good push would send it crashing into the valley.

Following Wes's lead, Andy got down on his hands and knees and crawled up behind it. Lying close to its side so that they were practically invisible, they looked over the top of the ridge.

Andy saw an open valley with a few trees and a creek meandering down the middle. On a knoll near the water was a camp of six tepees and a large cook tent. A number of horses grazed on the meadow, and others stood in a rope corral made from pack ropes tied to trees.

"There he is!" Andy whispered excitedly. "At the corral, the palomino."

Wes, looking through his binoculars, nodded without

speaking. Finally, he passed them to Andy. "Recognize anybody?" he asked.

Andy brought the glasses to his eyes and focused on a man walking away from the corral. He recognized Clint immediately. Then he picked out the cook tent and saw Heinie standing in the entrance with a dish towel in his hands. Other men were visible, but they were all new faces.

Andy told Wes about the men he recognized, but Wes shook his head. "I don't get it," he said. "There are too many men for the number of horses. How'd they get here?"

Andy still had the glasses to his eyes and saw the heavy man they had met the evening before come out of the cook tent to meet Clint. Under his arm he carried what looked like a submachine gun. He gazed up at the ridge, talking meanwhile with Clint. Then Garland joined them. There seemed to be an argument. Finally, Garland took the submachine gun away from the heavy man and disappeared into the tent again.

Andy gave a running explanation to Wes, who listened quietly, his face expressionless. "You can't shoot elk with a submachine gun," Wes said at last. "That's a close-range weapon. It's only used for—" His voice trailed off, but Andy knew what he meant. "It's only used for shooting *people*," he thought.

"I guess it's time to hold a little palaver." Wes started back toward the horses. "And you know," he went on, his voice powder-dry, "I think it's the first time in the Rockies a game warden ever faced a machine gun."

They rode down the ridge and across the meadow toward the camp. By the time they passed the rope corral and the saddled palomino tied to a tree, not a single man was visible. Following his uncle's lead, Andy dismounted, tied Sunny to an aspen, and walked toward the cook tent.

It was so quiet that he could hear the sound of the horses switching their tails in the corral. The flaps of the tepees were closed, flies buzzed over the dirty pack panniers strewn about the camp, and, though it seemed completely deserted, Andy could feel the eyes on him, following his every movement. There was a tension in the air, like the feeling just before a thunderstorm, Andy thought. His sweating skin clung to his cotton shirt. He felt his heart pumping. He remembered the dude with the automatic, the tough-looking men he had seen through the glasses only a few minutes before—and the submachine gun.

"We're outnumbered at least ten to two," he thought.

He looked up at his uncle walking beside him, unarmed. Wes's eyes flicked over the camp, taking in every detail. He didn't look scared; in fact, Andy thought maybe Wes was enjoying himself.

They stopped in front of the cook tent. Instead of shouting at the hidden eyes, getting action and, above all, breaking the tension as Andy wanted to do, Wes deliberately prolonged it. Casually, he turned his back on the cook tent, extracted a bag of tobacco from his shirt pocket, and rolled a cigarette. He licked the thin paper carefully and lighted the cigarette with a match taken from the band of his Stetson. He drew a long puff, then, turning, snapped the match through the tent flap.

"Come on out, Garland," he said in a conversational tone, "and bring your guide's license with you."

For a moment there was no answer, then Andy heard a movement in the tent, and Randy Garland parted the flaps and stood blinking in the sun. "What do you want?" he grumbled.

"Just checking up," Wes looked at Garland with the expression of a man examining a dead snake. "Where you keeping the meat?"

"What meat?" Garland stepped clear of the flaps, and Andy saw the heavy-set dude standing in the darkness of the tent, holding something behind him—the submachine gun, perhaps?

"The ranger reported shooting near here," Wes said. "And last night we found a dead doe near Big Game Creek. Know anything about it?"

"Nope." Garland gave Wes one of his mirthless grins. "I ain't heard no shootin'. An' we ain't plannin' to hunt till the season opens."

Andy heard movements behind them. He looked over his shoulder and saw men drifting out of the tepees—Easterners mostly, he thought, but tough-looking just the same. Some of them formed a group around Uncle

Wes, others seemed strangely interested in Sunny and Eighteen, and the rifles under their saddles.

"Cornered," Andy thought, looking at the pistols each man wore.

But Uncle Wes took no visible notice of the shuffling footsteps behind him. He simply stepped by Garland and looked into the cook tent at the mass of jumbled panniers, dirty dishes, and rumpled tarps. He completely ignored the big dude holding something behind his back.

"Well," he said with just a hint of sarcasm in his voice. "I'm glad to hear you're within the law for once, Garland. Now I want to see every hunting and guide license you have."

"What for?" Garland backed into the tent. "The season ain't open yet."

"No, but it will be in ten days, so you might as well get it over with."

When both men stepped into the open, Andy knew that his uncle had made an inventory of the tent with his eyes. If any meat was hidden there, it was cut into mighty small pieces.

Garland called to the men standing about the camp to bring their licenses, and each one passed in front of Wes with his permit to hunt. Andy knew, too, that each face was now engraved on Wes's memory. They were a grouchy lot, and for all their expensive Eastern riding clothes, a rough-looking bunch, kind of like the gangsters you see in the movies, Andy thought.

Clint, Heinie, and Garland showed their guide licenses, and when the last man's papers had been examined Garland asked, "You satisfied now, Marvin?"

Uncle Wes glanced over the group standing around him. "Not exactly," he said, quietly. "I just want to tell you men that you're the only pack outfit up here. If any game's killed before the season opens, you're guilty. Read your game laws, and remember that every elk or deer you kill has to be tagged before it leaves the country."

"Now you done?" Garland stuck his thumbs in his belt and stuck his chin out.

"Yes."

"Then get outa here before we throw you out. An' take your dirty little brat with you."

Wes smiled wryly. "Don't act tough for the boys, Garland," he said. "Maybe you better return that palomino before the sheriff finds it. And for the love o' Mike clean up this filthy camp before the ranger gets back."

He turned and elbowed his way through the group, with Andy close behind. They untied their horses and mounted. Uncle Wes looked down at the motley group below him and shook his head sadly. "Don't know what these mountains are coming to," he said. "Take some advice from an old-timer. Get rid of those city guns before somebody gets hurt."

He turned his horse and, with Andy beside him, rode toward the ridge.

When they were well out of earshot, Andy asked,

"What do you make of it, Uncle Wes? Have they been killing game?"

"Sure! They've hidden the meat somewhere. But the thing I can't figger is how all those Eastern bums got in here. They sure didn't ride in on those old pack-horse baits."

"And they didn't come in from Jackson Hole."

"No. I think Garland started toward the Hole to make people think he was heading away from the Big Game Creek country. Then he made a swing around, hoping nobody'd spot him. Looks like he cleaned out the Chicago gutters to find his dudes."

Dusk was falling when they arrived at the top of the ridge again. They turned their horses and looked down on the camp from the shadows of the forest. Uncle Wes used his glasses, but even without them Andy could see the activity in the meadow.

Clint, on the stolen palomino, was wrangling the horses away from the flat meadowland; his shouts and whistles drifted up to them in the still evening air. Then four other men started running across the meadow on foot, each one carrying a large white tarp.

"That's sure queer!" Uncle Wes murmured, keeping his glasses on them. "Can't figger what they're trying to do."

The heavy-set dude stood in the middle of the park and shouted at the others, pointing and giving directions.

Andy heard the faint humming sound first. It ex-

106

plained everything, immediately. "They're marking out a landing field for a plane, Uncle Wes," he said. "Hear it?"

Uncle Wes put down the glasses. "Well, I'll be doggoned!" He looked up at the deepening purple of the sky. "I might have known," he said. "They fly the men in and the meat out. The dirty robbers!"

The humming was distinct now. Twin motors, losing altitude fast, Andy thought. Then they saw it floating in from the north, a silver ship with only private license numbers on its tail. "An old DC-3," Andy said.

"I wouldn't know," Wes replied, shaking his head, ruefully. "When they start sending game wardens up in balloons, I'll have to resign." He watched as the pilot cut the motors and the plane slid in to a landing, bouncing unevenly on the improvised field marked off by the tarps. "I can read numbers, though," he said grimly. "And if it pulls out before I get to it, it's got to land somewhere."

"Gee," Andy said. "What'll we do now?"

Wes thought for a while, flipping the ends of his bridle reins idly against his leg. "If that thing was a horse," he grumbled, "I could figger what it would do. But you know more about planes than I do, Andy. If they all got in her and took on a lot of meat besides could she get off of there in the dark?"

Andy measured the length of the field with his eyes. Like most boys he was fascinated by planes. "It's possible, all right," he said. "But, gee, it sure would be dangerous taking off with a full load at night."

"O.K.," Uncle Wes turned his horse away from the valley. "These pack rats won't try to get out before daylight. We'll go back to camp. Turn the stock loose and grab some grub. I'll be back on this ridge before morning. I think maybe I'll send you out to the ranch with a message for the sheriff. Let's dangle, kid."

Andy slid Sunny down the trail behind Uncle Wes. It was rough going for the little horse in the gathering darkness, but as Andy watched Eighteen wallowing and plunging over the rocks, he was proud of Sunny's sure-footedness.

Eighteen was tired and feeling ornery. Wes slapped him from time to time across the cheek to make him turn. "I guess maybe this cayuse is just a jug-head," he said over his shoulder, pulling on the hackamore to make the horse take a switchback in the trail.

They were almost at the bottom of the ridge, riding along a steep cut bank over Big Game Creek, where the fast water rushed over boulders in the dark.

Uncle Wes turned to tighten a saddle string on his slicker, which had rubbed loose against a tree. Sunny was picking his way down the slope, so that Andy was above and behind Wes as they rounded a turn. Suddenly, in front of Eighteen, Andy saw a great black object, like a boulder, with two smaller black things behind it.

Then it moved. It reared suddenly, blocking the trail. Andy saw that it was a grizzly with two cubs.

He shouted a warning, and Uncle Wes, caught off

balance, started to straighten in the saddle. But Eighteen went crazy. The half-broken outlaw tried to turn on the narrow trail, then, seeing Sunny too close behind him, he plunged straight up, trying to climb the sheer cut bank itself.

Wes did his best to pull him down, and for a split second Andy thought he would succeed. The horse twisted on himself, trying to regain his balance. Then his hind feet slipped over the edge of the trail.

Uncle Wes shouted something and kicked his feet free of the stirrups. The horse fell sideways, screaming his terror, plunging, pawing the air as he went over the side. There was a dull thud of flesh on rocks, the sound of loose gravel sliding, and then silence.

Andy, sick at his stomach, sat paralyzed for a moment on a quivering Sunny. He felt the reins clammy in his hands. A great shiver went over him. Then he craned his neck at the dark water below. "Uncle Wes," he screamed. "Uncle Wes! You all right?"

"Uncle Wes—all right," an echo floated back, the only sound in an empty wilderness.

9

Andy Takes Command

~~~~~~

ANDY, HIS MIND IN A PANIC, LISTENED TO THE WATER rippling over the rocks. The gravel of the trail had ceased sliding. The faint whisper of the night wind in the pines was all around him.

Then Sunny tensed; his ears pricked forward. Andy heard scratching sounds, movements indefinable in the dark. The bear, the mother with two cubs! Sunny spun around in the trail and galloped back the way he had come.

Andy didn't try to stop him until they had left the cut bank and were well into a grove of aspens. Then he pulled up, listening. His teeth chattered. A cold fear chilled his body. All he heard was the dry rustle of the aspen leaves quivering in the breeze.

He didn't know how long he sat there, with Sunny moving restlessly under him. Gradually, the terror subsided. Little thoughts, sensible ones, began to filter through his mind. He wasn't alone. Sunny was with him. Sunny could outrun any bear in the world. Bears with cubs were dangerous, but only because they were defending their young. They wouldn't seek you out.

Andy got out his handkerchief and wiped his eyes and face. "Boy, I'm sure glad you're with me, Sunny," he said. His voice sounded damp and flat in the dark, but Sunny's ears flipped back, acknowledging the message, and, with a confidence that made Andy ashamed, began to crop quietly at the grass.

"Gee," Andy thought. "If he only knew how defenseless we are." Then he remembered the gun. Defenseless, my eye! He dismounted and drew the slim carbine from its scabbard. The icy feel of the barrel reassured him, and, as he slipped a cartridge into the chamber, each soft slide and click of the action added to his confidence.

In his own terror, he had almost forgotten Uncle Wes. Now, with a wave of shame, he wondered if his uncle was pinned under the horse, crying for help. Was he drowning, his head buried under the rushing waters of the creek?

For a moment, the sickness caught again at Andy's throat. He pressed his forehead against Sunny's neck to feel the reassuring warmth, and Sunny, remembering the nearness of a pants pocket that often carried carrots, nuzzled him carefully.

The thing to do was get back to Uncle Wes somehow—and fast! Get him out of the water. Look after him. "Here I am with a gun and a horse," he thought. "And all I do is stand here and shiver like a coward. A yellow, useless, coward!"

He thought of working his way to the creek bottom without going over the trail occupied by the bear, but decided that the deadfall timber was impassable. "Nope. I've got to cross that cut bank." He straightened up and raised the gun under his arm. "And if I meet that bear I'll just have to shoot her." He didn't dare ride. He was afraid that Sunny, with no gun training, might go crazy at the first shot.

Andy came out on the edge of the bank and felt the trail narrow under his feet. He had the feeling that he was walking through a grim nightmare, a dream that was repeating itself. There was terror ahead, yet he had to keep going; he had to face it.

Two things prodded him on: the thought of Uncle Wes somewhere below in the waters of the creek, and the warm breath on the back of his neck of the little horse behind him. Sunny, lonely too, crowded him just a little, anxious to get back to camp.

They reached the corner of the trail and Andy, poking the barrel of the carbine around it, strained his ears for the slightest sound. Nothing! No gravel slipping. He walked around the corner.

He could see the dark smudge of the trail where it dropped gradually across the cut bank toward the creek and the pine trees below. There was nothing on it. The bear must have turned and taken the cubs back down to the forest. Perhaps she was there, waiting.

He straightened and walked down the trail, shouting Uncle Wes's name. No one answered except the echo he had heard before, but it made him feel better. If the bear was down there waiting, he thought, if there was going to be a fight, it was best to alarm her and make her move around. He couldn't see anything in the timber. He'd have to shoot at the sound.

At the bottom, he faced a clump of pines, a wall of blackness between him and the creek. The terror was leaving him now. He shouted again as he entered the grove, his finger on the safety of his rifle.

Nothing moved. No sound came from the underbrush.

It was lighter on the creek bottom. The trees separated like the walls of a canyon, and the water reflected dull glints from the night sky. Andy left the trail and started up the creek toward the foot of the cut bank.

He scrambled over boulders and stepped knee-deep into pools. The water flushed over the tops of his boots until every step made a sloshing sound, and his sodden socks bunched painfully under his insteps. The high cowboot heels, so comfortable in the saddle, turned suddenly as they hit slippery stones, making his ankles ache.

Behind him, Sunny slithered over the boulders, his steel shoes clinking dully.

Once Andy fell and his rifle clanged against a rock. He picked himself up and put the gun back into its saddle scabbard. It was better to use the hand, he thought, and keep the other one tight on Sunny's reins.

113

If he met the bear out here on the creek bottom, he would have time to grab the carbine.

Slowly, his boots heavy with water, he made his way upstream. The thin, mountain air made him gasp for breath, and every few minutes he would slump onto a boulder to let his heart stop pounding.

When he finally came under the bank, Andy could see no sign of his uncle. Maybe he had gotten up and staggered away somewhere, or—Andy felt a catch at his heart—maybe the water had carried him down and they had passed him.

He stumbled along at the foot of the bank. Suddenly, Sunny snorted and reared. Andy, hanging grimly to the reins, was pulled over backward into the stream. The water surged over him and filled his eyes and nose. Coughing and spitting, he floundered desperately. He put out his hand to help himself up and felt something—something soft!

His heart jumped. He screamed and backed away, falling again on the slippery rocks.

Slowly he regained his feet, wiped the water from his eyes, and peered cautiously at the mound in front of him. It was Eighteen.

Holding a balky Sunny firmly, he prodded the body. If Eighteen were alive, he would kick and strike. But the head had hit a rock; the neck was twisted grotesquely. There was no sign of movement.

Andy circled the body to keep Sunny from rearing and began to examine the ground near by. If Uncle Wes was there at all, he couldn't be far. Andy remembered that his uncle had kicked his feet free of the stirrups. Otherwise he might have been pinned under the dead horse.

He found Wes close under the bank, lying with the back of his head in the water, his feet buried under rocks and gravel.

Andy dropped Sunny's reins and knelt beside his uncle. In the dark he could see no signs of injury. Frantically, he felt along Wes's arm to the wrist and tried to find the pulse. He wished he had taken a first-aid course and knew what to do.

The pulse was beating; he felt it faintly against his fingertips. He thought it was fast, perhaps, but he couldn't be sure.

When Andy stood up again, something brushed his face. Startled, he looked up and saw the roots of a long-dead tree above him. "Maybe that broke his fall," he thought. "I bet these good old roots saved his life."

Now what? Andy tried to remember what he had heard about accidents. You weren't supposed to move the patient until the doctor came, he thought grimly, in case the head was fractured or the back broken. It would be a long time before a doctor came to this creek.

He knelt down again and began to feel Wes's body. The arms seemed all right. He dug the legs from under the stones and gravel. Certainly the legs down to the boot tops weren't fractured. He was afraid to touch the head or to move the back.

Then Wes sighed and stirred. His eyes opened, and he raised himself slowly on his elbows.

"Uncle Wes!" Andy said softly. "Uncle Wes, you all right?"

His uncle sat up further, stared at him dully, then sank back again without speaking.

Andy felt tears in his eyes. His uncle didn't recognize him. Maybe he had a fractured skull.

Andy sat down in the sand and put his head in his hands. "I've got to get him out of here," he thought. "I've got to get him warm and comfortable."

He wondered whether he should go to Randy Garland's camp for help. Then he thought of the long trail in the dark, the tough men, the grin on Garland's face when he saw Wes's body.

"Nope. I've got to move him myself," he muttered. "His back isn't broken or he couldn't have sat up."

He examined the country up the creek and saw a bit of meadow near the shore. That was the place to get to, where he could make a fire.

He caught Sunny, who was pawing around among the boulders, led him to Wes, and tried to lift his uncle across the saddle. But Sunny kept sidling away, and the dead weight of a six-foot man was too much to lift. Andy found it easier to drag the body, and, after tying Sunny to a tree, he went to work.

The darkness took on its nightmare quality again as

116

he tugged Wes toward the park. Twice he fell, and, try as he would, his uncle's head was hard to protect from the rocks as, slithering and splashing, he finally reached the grassy bank.

He covered Wes with his slicker and an extra sweater from the back of his saddle and went in search of firewood.

A few minutes later and the first licking flames cast shadows against the trees. Andy piled on driftwood until a great arc of light surrounded them and the warmth began seeping through his soaked clothing.

For a while he tried chafing his uncle's wrists, but Wes never stirred. He was breathing easily though, Andy thought. His pulse seemed to be normal.

Finally, the great exertion at high altitude, the long day, and the lack of food began to tell on Andy, and the warmth of the fire crept through him like a drug. He built up the flames, then crept under the slicker next to Wes.

Now that he had no need of it, he saw the moon scudding between shreds of cloud. The night wind breathed on the pines, and an owl, its ghostly cry drifting from a distant ridge, mourned over something lonely and forgotten.

Andy drifted into the deep sleep of exhaustion. The fire died in glowing embers, and only Sunny, hungry and restless, saw the first steely dawn light.

"Andy!"

Andy struggled up through waves of weariness. Gradu-

117

ally he became aware of his aching muscles, of bruises and bumps and the hard ground beneath him. He opened his eyes and found himself looking at Uncle Wes.

"Uncle Wes! How you feeling? You all right?" Andy felt the life flowing back into him, but he watched Wes fearfully. Was he in his right mind?

Uncle Wes grinned ruefully and explored his head carefully with his fingers. "So far, all I feel is a big bump and I've got one walloping headache," he said. "What happened?"

Andy told him everything. When he had finished, Uncle Wes put a big hand on his shoulder. "Thanks, boy. You sure are a levelheaded kid," he said, simply. "I guess maybe you saved my life."

Andy couldn't think of anything to answer, but just the same the words made him feel mighty happy. "You get on Sunny, Uncle Wes," he mumbled, "and I'll climb on behind."

"O.K., boss." Wes threw back the slicker and started to his feet. His right foot gave way and he sank back on the grass, grunting with pain. "Bum ankle," he said through clenched teeth.

"Gee!" Andy knelt quickly by his side. "Is it broken, Uncle Wes?"

"Don't think so." Wes felt the swelling under the leather boot top gingerly. "I can move it if I have to. But you'll have to pack me back to camp."

Andy saddled Sunny, who was so hungry that it was hard to keep his head out of the grass. "Now you take it easy, Sunny," Andy said. "I want you to be very quiet and gentle as though you were taking out a little baby."

He led Sunny to a deadfall and tied him. Then he helped Wes to his feet. Wes put his right arm around Andy's shoulder, and they hobbled to where Sunny stood by the log. Slowly and painfully, Uncle Wes raised himself on it, throwing his weight on Andy's shoulder. He didn't speak. But Andy could see his face turn gray under his unshaven beard, and his breath came fast as he slowly reached for the saddle horn.

Andy crossed to the other side of Sunny and untied him. He was afraid that the pony might sidle away, letting Wes fall. But Sunny seemed to know that this was something special. He was carrying a delicate burden, and it was no time for mischief. He didn't move, and, while Andy talked to him quietly, Uncle Wes eased from the log into the saddle.

As Andy started to lead Sunny toward camp, he looked up at his uncle. Wes tried to smile back through gray lips, but his head sagged, he leaned on the horn, and he kept his right leg straight, free of the stirrup, as though the slightest movement was agony.

It wasn't far to the little cabin, but Andy made Sunny walk as slowly and gently as possible, and, when they finally crossed the meadow toward the corral, the sunlight was splashing the treetops.

Sunny nickered loud and long, and a great chorus answered him. The horses, held in the corral for almost

119

Uncle Wes leaned on the horn, and kept his right leg straig

of the stirrup, as though the slightest movement was agony.

—*Page* 119

twenty-four hours, were ravenous, and their calls for liberty and food battered at the ridges.

Andy led Sunny close to the corral poles and Wes used them to climb down. They stumbled to the cabin together, Wes leaning on Andy heavily until he could sink with a sigh of relief into the little wooden bunk against the wall.

When Andy slit the boot on the bad ankle with a jackknife and pulled it off, he saw Wes's face twist with pain.

"Now you take it easy," Andy said, pulling a blanket over him. "Pretty soon I'll be back with some cold compresses for that ankle and maybe it won't hurt so much."

Wes smiled at him faintly and closed his eyes.

Andy unsaddled Sunny and paused to consider which horse to use for wrangling. He knew that he should picket Snippy, but with Wes unable to ride and the possibility of the horses wandering where they would be hard to find, he hated to turn Sunny loose.

Sunny pulled at his bridle, saying plainly enough that it was time to start grazing. But Andy shook his head. "You're tough and you're fat, Mister," he said. "And I feel better when you're around. You better do your feeding on a picket rope." He tied the rope to Sunny's ankle and turned the other horses loose in the meadow.

The next few hours were the busiest of Andy's life. He lit the stove, cooked bacon and eggs, and brewed coffee for Uncle Wes. He put compresses on the bad ankle. He split wood, washed dishes, cleaned the camp, and finally, saddling Sunny, he rode back for Wes's saddle from the carcass of old Eighteen.

With Sunny again on the picket rope and Wes sleeping soundly, he sat down, his back to the cabin wall, and, basking in the sunshine, tried to plot out the future. Should he ride out for help immediately? How long would Uncle Wes's ankle keep him from the saddle? And if either of them left, what would Garland do? Butcher game to his heart's content? Andy decided that the best thing to do was talk it over with his uncle when he woke up. His head sank on his chest and he began to doze.

When Sunny whinnied, Andy's head snapped up.

Crossing the meadow, not more than a hundred yards away, was Randy Garland on his big gray.

10

Randy Garland Strikes

∞∞∞∞∞∞∞∞∞∞∞∞∞∞∞∞∞∞∞∞

*A*NDY SLIPPED INTO THE CABIN AND SHOOK WES BY the shoulder. He hated to wake him, but this was something he couldn't handle by himself. "Uncle Wes! It's Garland."

Uncle Wes opened his eyes and Andy was glad to see them sharpen with interest.

"Pull that blanket down, but leave it around my ankles. Act as though we dope around like this every day," he said, giving Andy a ghost of his regular grin. "Fool 'em if we can," he added, waving Andy toward the door.

Andy met Garland as he tied his horse at the corral. "Hello, bub," the man said, hoisting his chaps and giving Andy his toothy smile. "Your uncle around?"

Andy wondered why Garland was so cordial. Must want something, he thought. "He's in the cabin taking a nap," he answered.

Garland eyed him suspiciously. "Takin' a nap, huh? Why ain't he workin'?"

"The season isn't open yet, remember?"

Garland grunted, passed Andy, kicked the door open, and walked in, leaving Andy standing in the entrance.

Wes was propped up on a pillow, smoking a cigarette. The blanket lay loosely around his ankles, hiding the swelling. His face, still pale, was vague in the shadows of the windowless room. "Knock when you come in, Garland," he said dryly. "It's good manners."

But Garland ignored the suggestion. He showed his yellow teeth placatingly. "Now look, Wes," he said, leaning against the wall. "Maybe we better quit this here feudin'. It don't get us nowheres."

"I'm not feuding, Garland. You stay within the law and you won't have any trouble with me."

"The law's kinda foolish sometimes." Garland, trying to express himself, shifted his weight uneasily. "It ain't always fair."

Wes flicked a cigarette ash. "Why not?" he asked. Andy saw that Wes was leading him on, trying to find out what he was after.

"Well, us fellers that live here ought to be the ones to make a little cash out of hunters."

"That's right."

"An' maybe if we do a little quiet huntin' a coupla days before the season opens and the country crowds up, we shouldn't be watched too close."

"You better explain just exactly what you mean, Randy." Wes's voice was expressionless.

"Well, I got a proposition to make," Garland said. "These here dudes from Chicago have got plenty money,

125

but only a few days. They want to get their meat fast. Nobody but us knows for sure they're here." Garland paused, eying Wes shrewdly. "I got five hundred dollars in my pocket, Wes. You ride down as far as South Lake for a few days and it's yours."

"Five hundred bucks!" Wes snapped the butt of his cigarette at the stove. "That's a lot of money. You must be making plenty."

"I ain't doin' so bad." Garland smiled, encouraged by Wes's interest. "These boys are big shots. They play poker with thousand-dollar bills."

Wes leaned back against the pillow and locked his hands behind his head. "All I have to do is keep out of the way for a few days while you do your hunting and fly out the meat. But how're you going to find enough elk to make it worth while?"

"Don't you worry about that," Garland showed his teeth. "It ain't hard to locate elk from the air, signal the hunters, and go to shootin'!"

"It sounds like a good proposition, Randy." Wes's voice was casual.

"Then it's a deal, Wes. I'll help you pack."

"Get out," Wes said conversationally.

"Huh?"

"I said get out."

Garland's voice was cold. "Now look, Marvin. I ain't kiddin' about this. I give you your chance. Now you listen. These boys I got are tough. They was all for

126

pluggin' you yesterday an' tossin' you to the coyotes. I stopped 'em."

"That was very thoughtful of you."

"Yeah, but I ain't goin' to hold 'em again."

Wes sat up suddenly. "Look!" he said. "I don't give a hoot what you do. If you break the law I'm going to arrest you. And, frankly, it'll be a pleasure. Now take your dirty cash and get out of here."

But Garland didn't move. He was watching Wes closely, eying the blanket over his legs, the involuntary twinges of pain that crossed his face.

He leaned back against the wall and folded his arms. "Found a dead horse this morning," he said. "It carried your brand. Maybe you got bucked off."

"Maybe. But I'm still alive and I'm still game warden."

"Yeah?" Garland walked over and pulled the blanket from Wes's legs. He saw the bandaged ankle and he laughed. "Sure you're still game warden. But you're all stove up. You ain't good for nothin'."

The color flooded into Wes's face. He tried to get to his feet. But Randy reached out a big hand and pushed him back into the bed.

"You're under arrest right now, Garland," Wes said. "On your own evidence you've been hunting from a plane. I found the doe your dudes shot last night and—"

"Shut up!" Garland loomed over Wes now, his powerful fist drawn back to strike. "Nobody's goin' to arrest me. I'm flyin' out of here for good when this trip's over."

127

Andy didn't wait to hear any more. He streaked for his saddle at the corral, drew the carbine from its scabbard, and ran back to the cabin. For a moment, coming out of the bright sunlight, he was blinded. Then he could see the great bulk of Randy Garland standing over the bed.

He snapped the safety catch, raised the gun, and pointed it between Garland's shoulder blades. The barrel shook in his hands, but he steadied it against the door-frame.

"Leave my uncle alone," he said in a quavering voice.

Garland turned. His eyes grew big. His massive hands clenched. "Put down that gun," he said.

"I'll shoot," Andy said furiously. "You touch my uncle and I'll pump this gun till it's empty."

Andy heard his uncle laugh with a mixture of joy and relief. "There's tough boys in my camp, too, Garland," he said. "He's not kidding. He'll plug you."

Garland turned around slowly, and to Andy's surprise his hands went up. The thought flashed through Andy's mind that he should have yelled dramatically, "Hands up in the name of the law!" But what he said was, "Now I'm going to back away and let you out. But—but don't try anything. Get on your horse and go away."

Andy backed from the door and Garland walked through the entrance. He stood there for a moment, blinking in the sun, watching Andy to see if he really meant it. Then he turned his head and spoke over his shoulder.

"All right, Marvin," he said. "From now on things is goin' to be rough." He walked past Andy, who kept him covered until he had mounted his horse and ridden across the meadow.

When Garland had disappeared among the trees, Andy put the gun down. Now that it was over he felt his knees shaking. To stop them he walked into the cabin and sat down on the dirt floor.

"Well!" Uncle Wes said. "And I wasn't going to take you into the mountains for fear you'd be in the way! Mister, I just wish you were old enough to be a deputy. You could have put that rat in the hoosegow yourself."

Andy didn't feel like putting anybody in jail. The reaction had set in. He just wanted to sit there until he stopped quivering. "What do we do now?" he asked.

"That's going to take some thinking," Wes answered, and Andy could hear him trying to hide his weariness. "It looks to me as though maybe you'd better do as we planned and sneak out with a message to the sheriff. I need him and I need my deputies."

Andy was glad he had kept Sunny in. "O.K.," he said, wearily. "When do I start?"

"Early tomorrow morning. I don't want you on that narrow trail at night, and it's afternoon already." He smiled at Andy over the end of the bunk. "And anyway, you need some rest, boy."

But Andy was thinking. Who'd look after Uncle Wes while he was gone? Would Garland come back with his toughs and shoot him down? Outside the sun blazed at the open door. Andy saw a tiny chipmunk jerk across the ground, his eyes shining with mischief as he jumped on a pannier looking for food. Flies buzzed lazily, and in the distance Andy could hear the occasional deep bong of Jug's bell as he switched at a deerfly.

"What'll you do for food, Uncle Wes?" Andy asked.

"Well, maybe you better cook up some grub before you go," Wes said. "But don't worry about me. I'll move my bed to the door. I don't think these fellers will attack me. They know I can still shoot."

They sat in silence for a time, then, without warning, Wes sat up suddenly.

"What's the matter?" Andy asked.

"Shhh!" Wes cupped his ear with his hand.

Andy listened intently, trying to hear something new, but, except for the sound of Jug's bell, which was ringing more frequently, he heard nothing unusual.

Then the bell began to ring wildly.

"Hop on your horse, Andy," Wes said, a furrow in his brow. "And take a look at the horses. It may be flies making them restless and then again it may be—"

Andy didn't wait to hear the rest of the sentence. He was out the door and headed for Sunny. He took off the picket rope, saddled, and came back to the cabin for the binoculars hanging from a nail on the wall.

He stopped in his tracks and listened for a few seconds.

The sound of the bell was growing fainter. "The horses must be moving right along," he thought.

As he grabbed the glasses, Wes's voice stopped him. "Andy, you'd better trail 'em carefully just in case you should run into our friends. Ride the ridge behind the cabin here first and use the glasses."

"O.K., Uncle Wes."

"And, Andy! Don't take any chances. Remember the most important thing is to get on that trail for the ranch tomorrow morning."

Andy climbed the ridge behind the cabin, pushing Sunny as fast as he dared over the rough ground. When he reached the top, he saw why his uncle had sent him there. In every direction he could see for miles across the parks and creek bottoms. He dismounted, sat on a rock, and put the glasses to his eyes.

Starting from where he thought the horses had been grazing, he played his glasses over each opening in the timber. Once he thought he had found them, but a careful examination showed instead a small herd of elk grazing in the shadow of the pines.

Magpies squawked in the aspens. The haze from a distant forest fire lay along the ridges. Andy felt discouraged. Things were happening too fast for him, he thought. It sure was time to get some help.

The air stirred slightly. A tiny puff of wind blew against his ear, and with it came the distant sound of a bell. Andy stopped breathing. Even his heartbeats

131

were loud as he strained to catch the direction of the sound.

It seemed to come from the ridge between him and Lost Basin. He looked for the cut bank, the scene of last night's adventure. When he found it, he tried to follow with the glasses the trail that led up the ridge.

The bell was more distinct now. Slowly he raised the glasses until he saw a dry gulch, an open seam in the ridge where the trail crossed a dry creek bottom.

There they were! A buckskin—that would be Punkin —followed by a bay. Jug, no doubt. Then came Tarbaby, the roan, and Snippy.

And behind them?

Andy drew a sharp breath. He saw a man on a coffee-and-cream colored horse. There was no doubt of it. That was Clint on the stolen palomino.

11

Through Enemy Lines

~~~~~~~~~~~~~~~~~~~~~~~~~~~~~~~~~~~~~~

*B*Y THE TIME ANDY HAD CROSSED THE CREEK AND started up the Lost Basin trail he thought he must have gained considerably on Clint and the horses, and he remembered Wes's warning, "Don't take any chances!"

He was riding by himself into the enemy's country. Should he stop and go back, he wondered, and let them hide the pack string?

Undecided, he pulled Sunny up. It would be safer to keep away from Lost Basin, he thought. But he was curious. Suppose he followed Clint to some hidden spot where the horses were allowed to graze. Sooner or later, Clint would leave and he could wrangle the cavvy back to Uncle Wes in triumph. If he could just peek over the ridge into the open basin he was bound to see where they were going.

Then Andy remembered the big chimney rock he and Uncle Wes had hidden behind the day before. He'd have a look from there. He turned off and worked Sunny through the brush.

He was on a sidehill, out in the open, when the plane

133

roared over the ridge. Andy felt pinned like a fly under a microscope. There was no cover, no use making a run for it. He held Sunny up, trying not to move as the plane's shadow crossed them. He was conscious of his blue shirt, of Sunny standing golden in the sunshine. The plane, a flash of silver, bore away to the south.

Andy ran Sunny into the aspens and waited. Would they come back for another look? He heard the motors, fainter, then louder, but it didn't return. A few minutes later he saw it circling at a higher altitude. "Looking for game," he thought.

Andy tied Sunny to an aspen and climbed the ridge on foot. If they had seen him there was nothing he could do about it now. But he knew that the crew of a plane moving fast on the take-off and still close to the ground might easily miss the tiny figure of a boy on a horse.

He reached the top and peeped over the edge, then ducked back, flattening himself into the ground. A few feet to his left, two riders had pulled up and were staring out over Lost Basin. One of them was Garland.

Andy dug his nails into the ground. Cold sweat poured off him, making his shirt stick to his body. "Well," he heard Garland say. "Clint's got Wes Marvin's pack string. Now we ain't got nothin' to worry about at all."

"Yeah? Don't be too sure!" said another voice. "How about that kid? He's still got a horse. He'll ride out for help."

Andy felt his ears sticking out like pitchers.

"Don't worry none about that, Big Joe," Garland answered. "I got Heinie on the mouth of Pass Creek waitin' for him."

"Maybe the kid'll ride around him."

"Nope. Trail runs across a cut bank. Creek on one side. Bank on the other. Hey, let's go! We gotta get that meat shipped before dark."

Their voices faded as they rode away, but Andy still hugged the ground. So that was the plan, he thought. They had planted Heinie on the mouth of Pass Creek to catch him when he tried to ride out for the sheriff. Well, Uncle Wes would tell him how to get around that cut bank. By golly, he'd do it some way.

Once more, keeping flat to the ground and close to the chimney rock, he peered over the ridge.

As he raised his head, he saw Clint and the pack string headed up the little creek toward the head of the basin. That was worth knowing, Andy thought. The chances were he could find the horses if he ever had the opportunity.

But what was Garland doing? Andy raised his head further and looked below him. Garland and the heavy-set dude called Big Joe were joining two other riders, who were driving eight pack horses loaded with sides of meat. They were headed toward the camp on the knoll.

Andy ducked his head down to think it over. They were getting ready to load the plane. Somewhere, not very far from where he was lying, was the place where

135

He saw Clint and the pack string headed toward the head of the basin.

Garland hid his illegal meat, and that was what Uncle Wes wanted to know about most of all.

If only he could find it! Andy felt excitement rising in him. He forgot to be scared. Somewhere down deep in him he heard his uncle's words again, "Don't take any chances."

But this was a chance worth taking, wasn't it? This would wrap the whole thing up. It completed the evidence. If he could get this information out to the sheriff, it would keep Garland and the rest of them out of this country forever.

He looked over the ridge again, trying to figure out where Garland's pack string had come from. He'd heard the voices first on his left, he thought, and now the horses were entering the camp in the middle of the basin off to his right. Andy wished he could look for tracks, but that would make him an obvious target.

He examined the country to his left and saw a large grove of pine about a half mile away. The ridge above it looked steep, and there were outcroppings of rock forming a jagged line of cliff.

It was in that grove somewhere, Andy thought. If he crawled along behind the ridge until he got to the trees, he could get down under that cliff and look for tracks.

Andy reached the timber easily enough, but once in the trees the going was slowed by great jagged rocks, deadfalls, and high bushes. Andy clambered over stumps,

137

circled the crumbling cliffs, and slid down steep banks of rubbly pudding stone.

Finally, after wading through a thicket of juniper, he hit a rough trail. He examined it carefully and saw hoofmarks, a lot of them, headed both ways. He followed them deeper into the timber.

Andy kept looking for a cabin or a tent, but the trail wandered on over dead trees and around boulders fallen from the cliffs above. Then it turned toward the cliff, went on for a hundred feet or so, and stopped in a little dell.

Andy circled to see if he could pick up the trail again, but judging from the way the grass was trampled, this was the end of it and the pack horses had been tied here.

He examined with his eyes the sheer wall of rock and the bushes and saplings in front of it. Some of the brambles were broken. He pushed through the bushes to the foot of the cliff.

Then quite suddenly he found himself facing a door set directly into the face of the rock. It was new, made of hand-hewn logs set in an old frame, but amazingly well concealed, Andy thought.

He opened it and walked inside. A cave ran back into the rock for what Andy estimated must be a hundred feet. Probably some old prospector had started a mine there, he thought. Uncle Wes had told him about the old-timers who still roamed the hills looking for gold.

It was cool and dry, and the rubble had been cleared to one side. The old stanchions that supported the roof had been shored up for safety. What interested Andy most, however, were the rows of hooks set into the wall. From several of these hung great haunches of meat ready for shipment.

Andy was examining a carcass, wondering whether it was that of a deer or an elk, when he heard a faint thudding sound.

He held his breath and listened. Was there something in the cave, an animal, perhaps? He looked around nervously. There it was again, a rhythmic sound.

Suddenly he realized he was listening to hoofbeats. Some fault in the earth, some underground fissure, was warning him. Garland and the dude were coming back.

Andy ran to the door, flung it open, and had just time to duck into the brush. He felt like plunging through it regardless of noise or the trail he left behind him. But he held himself back and slipped as silently as he could through the tangled thickets.

Once he hesitated, wanting to stop and listen again to the voices of Garland and the dude. He could hear the pack horses lumbering up the trail. But dusk was falling and he had the information he needed, so he kept moving, putting each foot down carefully where it would make the least noise, slinking like a coyote through the timber and taking advantage of every tree and bush.

When he finally reached the other side of the ridge, he sat down on a grassy bank to catch his breath and

139

think things over. It was all up to him now, he thought. He and Sunny were responsible for catching these men.

A sudden puff of wind chilled him. Looking westward, he saw great piles of cloud, black and cold-looking, banking up and hiding the red of the sunset.

He remembered the warm sweater on the back of his saddle and stood up stiffly. "Better get going," he thought. "Weather's changing and I've got to get rest and food, and Uncle Wes has to tell me how to avoid the mouth of Pass Creek."

In the grove of aspens where he had tied Sunny, the leaves touched by frost shivered like yellow coins in the wind, and some were drifting down through the dusk. It looked different with the leaves on the ground, Andy thought vaguely. He came to the place he thought Sunny should be but saw no sign of him.

"That's queer," he thought, and suddenly his heart began to sink. "This looks like the place. Gee, I must be tired! I'm losing my grip."

He began a systematic circle of the grove, but as the clouds moved up the sky and the light faded, the trees lost their detail. Wherever he stopped, the slim trunks stood in irregular rows, and each might well have been the one Sunny had been tied to.

Andy felt the panic growing in him, the fear of the man who is suddenly alone in the woods. Maybe this was the wrong grove! Maybe Sunny had broken loose! "Sunny!" he called. "Sunny!"

He listened for the sound of restless hoofs or Sunny's

soft nicker. The horse should be hungry by now; he should be anxious to be turned loose to graze. But all he heard was the dry rustle of the aspen leaves falling before the wind.

Desperately, Andy circled the grove again. Once more he came to the place where he thought he had tied Sunny. This time he examined the ground, looking for tracks, but the fallen leaves and the fading light made tracking impossible.

Then a glint of something metallic caught his eye. He walked over and picked it up. It was Sunny's bit. The reins, still tied to the tree, had slipped down the slender trunk, and the bridle itself was lying behind a stump.

He examined the throatlatch. It was still buckled, as though the horse had rubbed his head against the tree until he had scraped the headstall over his ears and freed himself.

Andy knew that old Jug was adept at that very thing, and had pulled a halter loose many times. But Sunny! He'd never done anything like that.

Andy sat down on the stump, feeling more lonesome than ever before in his life. It was one tough thing to lose the horses to Clint, but to lose Sunny! That was more than he could bear.

Andy put his head in his hands. Maybe Sunny's pulled loose by himself, he thought. But it would be easy for someone to pull the headstall off and rebuckle the throatlatch.

If that plane had seen him and signaled the camp,

141

somebody could have come over the ridge while he was at the mine and turned Sunny loose.

A wave of anger rolled over Andy. It was bad enough to steal game, but to take a man's horse, to sneak it away—

It was a smart trick, too. No one could accuse you of horse stealing, if the horse was wandering around loose with the saddle on.

Andy stood up, tightened his belt, and swore that he'd find Sunny if he had to stay in the mountains all winter.

But turned loose, where would Sunny go? Back to camp, maybe? He'd fed the horse carrots there. Andy felt a momentary thrill of optimism. The thing to do was get back fast, before it was completely dark. Maybe he'd find his horse grazing on the meadow in front of the little cabin.

With this vision before him, Andy jammed his hat over his eyes and trotted down the hill, slipping and sliding until he reached the trail.

The sky was completely overcast and the wind was still rising when he reached the edge of the park and saw a pinprick of light from the door of the little cabin.

He stopped short and looked around the meadow. There was no sign of his horse, but maybe it was too dark to see him.

Listening with all his might, he heard no sound of a pony pulling grass, no gentle thump of hoofs on turf.

He started toward the cabin, his feet dragging with

142

weariness. Somehow, the whole adventure fell flat without Sunny to share it.

He was halfway across the meadow when a voice snapped, "Pull up there! Who are you?"

"Uncle Wes," Andy shouted. "It's Andy!"

"Come on in, kid." The door opened wider, and Andy saw Uncle Wes sitting on his bedroll inside, his rifle across his lap. He made room for Andy to enter.

"Uncle Wes, is Sunny here?" Andy blurted. "Did he come home?"

"Sunny?" Uncle Wes looked puzzled. "Why, you were riding him. For Pete's sake, you haven't let him get away, have you?"

Suddenly, Andy realized how completely he had disobeyed his uncle's instructions. He'd taken chances. He'd lost the last of the horses. That left Garland free to do as he pleased. A wave of shame flooded over Andy as he sank down next to the red-bellied stove.

"Oh, Uncle Wes," he groaned. "I've ruined everything!" And he told his uncle of his afternoon's adventures.

Uncle Wes listened without expression, fingering his swollen ankle from time to time. When Andy had finished, Wes lit a cigarette and inhaled a long puff.

"Well," he said finally. "That's that!"

"I've been an awful dope, Uncle Wes," Andy said. "I–I didn't realize about Sunny being the last horse. I mean—there was a chance to find out where they kept the meat and—" His voice trailed off miserably.

143

Uncle Wes smiled. "Take it easy, kid," he said. "If I'd seen that meat, I'm pretty sure I'd have done the same thing."

Andy breathed a sigh. Uncle Wes could sure take it! "I'm to blame, just the same," he said.

Uncle Wes shook his head. "Nope!" he said. "That old mother bear with two cubs is to blame. And that jug-headed Eighteen. And look at me! I've been in the mountains for thirty years, and here I go getting bucked off, piled up in a creek bottom with game rustlers all over the country. And you say *you* make mistakes!"

Andy knew his uncle was just trying to keep his spirits up, but just the same he couldn't help feeling a little better.

He got up and took off his blue jeans, wet from crossing Big Game Creek, and hung them near the stove. If his uncle was still in there pitching, he shouldn't mope around either.

"What do we do now, Uncle Wes?" he asked wearily.

"I'm afraid we're washed up for the time being," Wes replied. "Garland and his gang shipped the meat tonight. I saw the plane flying east just before sunset."

"You mean—" Andy looked incredulous. "You mean you're giving up?"

"No." Wes shifted his bad ankle painfully. "I'll catch Garland later and use your evidence, but there's nothing more I can do now."

Andy peeled off his shirt. "Gee," he said. "We've got to do something. We can't let 'em go on killing elk.

144

Just butchering 'em." His crestfallen face appeared under the shirttail and he looked at Uncle Wes accusingly.

Wes smiled affectionately. "You think I'm quitting?" he asked.

"No. But—but—"

"Look, Andy," Wes said. "If you have any ideas, shoot! But remember this! We're afoot. We're outnumbered. We're dealing with rats. And the weather's changing. Listen to that wind."

Outside, the wind stirred the pines and moaned wearily around the cabin. Andy shivered and climbed into flannel pajamas.

"What'll we do?" he asked.

"If my leg gets well in time, we'll walk out and get help. If not, we'll wait for the deputies to come in and get us."

Andy pondered this while he slapped some ham into the frying pan and added two eggs. The snapping grease, the delicious smell roused him.

"Hey!" he said suddenly. "I'll walk out and get help tomorrow."

For the first time, Wes really grinned. He slapped his good leg. "By golly, I hoped you'd say that!" he said. "And I just wondered if you would."

"Sure!" Andy burst out. "I'll take off first thing in the morning. I'll call Sally from the ranger station, and she'll get the sheriff, and—"

"Whoa there!" Uncle Wes held up his hand. "I didn't say you were going. You're not. I wouldn't let my brother's boy wander around these hills in a storm. Why, you might get lost, or hurt, or catch pneumonia. Or for that matter you might get shot. You're more important than herds of elk."

"But—" Andy tried to interrupt.

"No, Andy! Remember that Heinie is waiting at Pass Creek."

"Well, I'll circle Pass Creek."

"No, Andy. It's not worth the risk."

Andy waved his arms. He flourished his knife and fork, arguing between mouthfuls of ham and eggs. He almost beat his chest to show how tough he was. His shadow danced on the walls of the cabin, as he argued for a chance to keep up the fight.

Uncle Wes watched and listened. Finally he said, "You're a tough kid, Andy. All right, I'll let you go. On two conditions."

"Anything you say, Uncle Wes. Just give me my chance."

"If it really starts to storm before you get over the divide, you must come back. If you meet any of Garland's men, you must not put up a fight. Do exactly as they tell you, or you'll get hurt. O.K.?"

Andy drew a deep breath. "O.K.," he said.

12

Capture

~~~~~~

AFRAID THAT A STORM HAD BROKEN, ANDY CRAWLED out of his sleeping bag at dawn and peered through a crack in the door. The grass glistened, the trees dripped, and the gray clouds hung on the Lost Basin ridge. But it wasn't storming; the wind had gone down. He looked for Sunny, hoping he had come into the meadow during the night, but there was no sign of him.

"I don't think Sunny'll come back here," said Uncle Wes, reading Andy's mind. "He wasn't here long enough to get located. He might drift home, but most likely he'll hunt up the rest of the cavvy. Ponies don't like to be left alone."

"Will he be all right with that saddle on?" Andy asked.

"I think so," Wes said. "If it slips on him he'll kick it to pieces, probably. But there's no bit in his mouth. He'll get plenty to eat."

After filling himself with a stout breakfast of stewed apricots, bacon, eggs, hotcakes, and a cup of boiling hot coffee, Andy prepared for his trip.

Capture

He wore his thick California pants and a flannel shirt.
His sweater was tied on the back of Sunny's saddle, but
he had a good leather windbreaker, and his uncle gave
him a woolen vest to go under it. He exchanged his
cowboots for a pair of tough leather shoes. High cowboot heels were no good on a long hike. He stuffed
extra socks into his pocket.

For food he took several big slabs of cheese, a hunk
of bread, a small can of condensed milk, and several
chocolate bars.

"Doggone it!" Uncle Wes gazed furiously at his ankle.
"If only I could go with you, we'd have these birds in
jail by the end of the week. Remember, Andy, as soon
as you get the message through, go right to the ranch
and go to bed. You'll be more tired than you've ever
been in your life. Don't try to come back here. The
sheriff'll look after everything."

"How long'll this trip take, Uncle Wes?"

"You can't make it in one push in this altitude, Andy.
Don't try. Take a lot of rest. And when you get over
the divide, stop off at a little dugout off the trail to
your right."

Uncle Wes traced the trail with a burnt stick on a
piece of tarp. "You can't get lost except in a big storm.
Trail's well marked by the Forest Service, and you've
been over it before. Now, here's how to get around the
mouth of Pass Creek." He showed Andy where to leave
the trail, cross a high butte, and then drop back to the

trail again. "But remember. If you're caught by those men, do as they say. Play the dumb kid."

"That won't be hard," Andy said, wryly. "Not after yesterday."

Uncle Wes struggled up on his good leg and leaned in the doorway. "Probably I'm the stupid one to let you go," he said. "But you've got spunk. And if these men are caught, you'll get the credit."

"Phooy on that!" Andy grinned. "Those guys took my horse!"

They shook hands. "Go to it, boy," Wes said.

Andy crossed the meadow, but before he entered the forest he took a last look back. Wes was still leaning in the doorway. Andy felt a wave of affection for him. It sure was tough for him to be out of the fight, he thought. Darn tough!

He plunged into the woods and soon found that he was walking too fast. His heart was pounding and on even a little rise of ground he found himself blowing like a walrus. He slowed up and tried to keep a steady pace, resting every twenty minutes or so.

The clouds hung low and the air was chill and damp, but Andy found himself sweating mightily under his flannel shirt. He took off his windbreaker and vest and tied them around his waist. Then he came to the first creek crossing.

There was high swamp grass on either bank. Andy took off his shoes, rolled up his trousers. and plunged in, grateful that the water was low.

149

He was wading through the tall grass on the far side, when he heard something plunging toward him. He jumped off the trail, ducked down in the mucky ooze, and tried to stop breathing.

It sounded like a horse coming down the stream. "Maybe it's Heinie," he thought. "He's changed his camp site and is waiting for me here."

The grass hid Andy, but as he peered between the tall stems he could see where his own footsteps approached. He would be easy to find, he thought bitterly. Perhaps this was the end already, even before he'd got started.

The sounds came nearer. Something was battering its way through the stiff grass, pulling its feet from the mud with great sucking sounds.

Andy lifted his head a few inches higher and saw a bulk lunging toward him. Great flat prongs waved through the grass. Then a bull moose stepped into the creek bottom and, sensing an enemy, stopped and turned his head. A pendant of flesh, like a bell clapper, swung from his neck, as he gazed solemnly at where Andy was hiding.

Andy stepped into the trail. "Scram, moose!" he said. "There's a bunch of bums around here who'll murder you on sight."

The moose stared at him with ridiculous dignity, as though weighing his words, then, evidently thinking there must be some truth in them, he trotted with great loping strides into the timber.

Capture

An hour later, when Andy saw the butte rising from the valley, he knew that he was approaching Pass Creek, and he began to travel as silently as possible. He listened to the slightest sound, even the dripping of the trees and the occasional damp squawk of a magpie. Finally, he cut off the trail to his left into the thick timber.

It was afternoon by the time he reached the top of the butte, but it was worth it, he thought, as he lay on his stomach and gazed down at the mouth of Pass Creek. He couldn't see the trail across the cut bank, but he didn't need to, because directly below him Heinie's campfire smoldered in a park.

Andy felt a little like a god, sitting up there in the clouds. He thought he could almost touch the gray sky above. Below him from time to time bits of scud blew gently across his line of vision. He felt superior to Heinie, who was cooking something in a skillet over the fire.

"By this time," Andy thought, "Mr. Heinie knows I'm afoot. He probably isn't worrying about me much. I wonder what he'd think if he knew I was staring down on his suspender buttons right now!"

Andy stretched out his legs and ate some chocolate and some bread and cheese. It was fun to eavesdrop on a man who was hunting you. He was enjoying himself thoroughly when he felt the first drop of rain.

Was that a storm coming? Andy jumped up. If he wasn't at the divide by the time the storm broke, he'd promised to return to the cabin.

151

He plunged into the timber again.

By the time he had crossed Pass Creek a mile above its mouth and broken through the timber back to the trail, the rain was coming down in a fine drizzle. Andy put on his jacket, but the fine drops filtered down his neck and the mud of the creek bottom clung to his trousers.

"But you couldn't call it a *storm*," Andy thought. "That is, not a real one. No trees are being blown over."

He kept plugging along, but his bones ached with weariness. It was steady uphill climbing, and each time he reached a ridge top he expected to see the pass in front of him, but, as the flat grayness of the cloud ceiling began to grow black, he still hadn't reached the timber line.

Life seemed to consist of plugging up hills, through timber, across little parks, then through more timber until you reached a ridge top. You looked over it eagerly, to find more parks, more timber, then a creek to cross.

He had long ago decided that his feet were so wet that there was no use removing his shoes to cross water.

He remembered in a dreary way how long the trip had seemed to him when they rode in, and he thought of how easy it really was to sit in a saddle and let old Sunny do the work.

Sunny! The only way to get him back was to keep walking! He plodded on.

By the time it was almost dark, Andy felt that he must be near the divide. He could no longer see much from the ridges, but Big Game Creek had dwindled to a brook, a sure sign, and he could jump across most of its branches.

At the edge of a tiny meadow he saw a great pine tree with an inviting bed of needles underneath. He sank down wearily and found that the hundreds of branches above had kept the ground almost dry. He took off his shoes, dried his feet with a handkerchief, and put on dry socks. There were blisters on his heels and his toes were numb with cold. He rubbed them briskly.

He jammed a hole in the can of condensed milk with his knife, made some cheese sandwiches, and ate the cold mess wearily. He wasn't hungry. He was too tired for that, but he thought food might give him the energy to go on.

He leaned back for a moment against the tree trunk. It wouldn't do to go to sleep, he thought. Had to cross the divide first—find that cabin dug into the mountain-side. He fell into fitful slumber.

He dreamed of climbing everlasting hills, of creeks that opened out suddenly in front of him. Then he was taking his shoes off. It took a long time because the knots were wet, and he should be watching the trail because—because there were noises—coming nearer—

Andy woke with a start. Terror gripped him. Had he really heard something?

And where was he? In front of him was an expanse of white. Except for a little circle surrounding the

153

tree, the ground was covered with snow. Great wet flakes drifted down, making everything look strange and different. He sat up and let the memories of the previous day flood over him.

Then Andy heard the sound. There was no mistake this time!

He ducked behind the tree and lay flat on his stomach. Somebody, something was coming up the trail. The snow threw up a little light against the trees, but it muffled sound. There it was again!

Andy riveted his eyes on the spot where the trail entered the meadow. His mind raced. Of course! They'd seen his tracks. They knew he was trying to get out. They were after him.

Andy was grateful for the carpet of white that surrounded him. There was no sign of his own trail in it. Perhaps they would go by without seeing him. In this snow, ideal for tracking, they'd soon wonder why he left no footprints.

Branches crackled, then something, a black shape, appeared at the entrance of the park. Andy held his breath. It certainly moved slowly.

It ambled into the meadow, a black bulk, strangely out of shape.

Suddenly, as it stepped into the whiteness, Andy saw it was a horse, with a slipped saddle halfway down its side.

"Sunny," he yelled.

154

Sunny jumped as though struck by a rattler and dove back into the grove.

Andy ran from behind his tree, calling himself names. Here was Sunny, saddle and all. He hadn't been able to find the pack string and had struck out for home. Now he was crashing through the woods, trying to circle the park, scared stiff by the sudden, stupid shout.

Andy ran up the trail. There was a chance, a tiny chance! The woods were thick along here; they'd force Sunny back on the trail sooner or later.

Andy kept moving until he came to an open sidehill. He crossed it, took up his post where the trail entered the timber again, and waited.

It was hard not to move, not to call out, but, until he knew exactly where Sunny was, it would be useless. Even though Sunny was becoming a pet, the chances of catching a mustang at night in the open country are a hundred to one.

Andy waited for what seemed hours. Finally, just as the suspense was becoming unbearable, Sunny's head peered cautiously out of the timber.

This time Andy spoke softly. "Sunny! Hey, Sunny! Carrots!" Desperately Andy searched his pockets. He hadn't been wearing his California pants much, but down in one corner in the lining of the pocket were a few grains of oats. He put them into the palm of his hand. "Hey, Sunny, oats!" he called gently.

Sunny held his ground, his ears pricked forward, and

155

Andy felt he could almost read his mind. "Was it really the boss? What was he doing out here? Doggone it! He said oats!" Sunny stepped into the open, ready to jump away in a split second.

Andy took a few steps toward him. Sunny backed away.

Andy's heart sank. Uncle Wes had warned him how horses change in the hills. When they were away from their home corrals, living in the wilds, it was much harder to make pets of them.

Once again, Andy stepped forward, speaking softly. Sunny snorted, spun on his heels, and ran back to the edge of the woods.

For a second, Andy wanted to run after him, but he knew that would send the horse crashing through the brush again. Andy stayed where he was and rolled the oats in his hand, trying to make the grains crackle.

The horse came out of the timber, trotting high, blowing through frosty nostrils. His mane was powdered with snow, and the saddle, askew on his back, annoyed him. Every few steps he stopped and kicked at the stirrup slapping against his belly.

"No wonder he's spooky," Andy thought, "with that saddle all over his back." Even the blanket had slipped over his rump, and Sunny could feel it flapping every time a puff of wind lifted its folds.

Sunny was annoyed. But he also had sensitive ears, and crackling oats meant something very good indeed.

He took a few more steps and began to stretch his neck out, trying to make his nose reach Andy's hand.

Andy opened his palm, hoping Sunny could see the oats, and brought it closer to his body. Using his other hand, he unbuckled his belt and pulled it loose from his Californias.

This was too much for Sunny; he jumped away again.

Andy groaned. Here he was, standing in the middle of the Wyoming Rockies at night, trying to catch a horse in a snowstorm. Yeah, and if he didn't watch it, his pants would fall off!

He felt foolish but he kept talking and crackling the oats. Once again Sunny approached, craning his neck, pushing his little blazed nose out until it almost touched Andy's hand.

This time, Andy was more careful. Keeping the belt behind his back, he pulled the hand holding the oats against his body. Sunny was forced to take a step forward. The oats were so close he couldn't resist them. Andy felt the wonderful mushy softness of the horse's nose nuzzle the palm of his hand.

Carefully, he brought the belt around to Sunny's mane while the horse scooped up the few kernels of grain. Then Andy let the belt drop across the neck.

Sunny snorted, leaned back, ready to spin away. Andy patted the underside of the neck, then slowly slipped the end of the belt through the buckle.

Sunny was caught.

Capture

Andy heaved a great sigh. The world suddenly seemed to brighten. The snow was a beautiful thing to behold; the ridges, the never-ending trail, the mud of the creek bottoms were something to gallop over. The loneliness had gone, too, the feeling of being a tiny speck lost among empty mountains. You couldn't be alone when your arms were around the swellest little mountain pony in Wyoming.

Andy took off his rope from the twisted saddle and fashioned a headstall, as Sally had once showed him, and although it wasn't a very neat job, he thought it would do as a hackamore. Then, unsaddling, he felt over Sunny's back, looking for sores. He found the hair rubbed off in spots, but the skin wasn't broken and there was no swelling. He refolded the blanket carefully and saddled up.

"Sunny," he said, "let's scram."

Somehow the rest of the ride took on a dreamlike quality for Andy. He gave the pony his head, and Sunny, the home corral in mind, knew exactly what to do. As soon as they were over the divide, he broke into a slow dogtrot. If Andy hadn't been so weary he might have thought how dangerous it was to trot down a narrow trail in the dark with only a foot of slimy mud between you and a rocky canyon.

The steep switchbacks made the horse bunch his legs so close together that the hind ones were within inches of the front. He slid and scrambled, but he held the pace, and Andy, swaying in the saddle, was only too glad to turn everything over to the horse's judgment.

As they dropped to a lower altitude the snow changed to rain again. It filtered through the windbreaker and down his back, but Andy, leaning on the pommel, hardly noticed it.

The horse stopped, and Andy straightened up and looked about him. He realized that he must have been dozing in the saddle because the trail had ended and they had reached the valley of the South Fork. A leaden dawn lay along the peaks. In front of Sunny was the first gate with a sign on a post reading, "South Fork Ranger Station, 1 mile."

Andy opened the gate and rode on. There was just one more thing to do, he thought. Call Sally. Wake up long enough to give her every detail of the situation, every single thing that might be important to the sheriff.

Then he'd go to sleep for a week.

He yelled as he galloped up to the little house with a four-sided roof and a chimney sticking up in the middle of it. "Hey!" he hollered. "Hey, Mr. Ranger!"

No one answered. Andy dismounted wearily and hammered on the door. It was securely padlocked. Every window was boarded up. Tacked to the wall was a message, neatly typed, "Gone to fight fire in the North Fork. Hold mail at Marvin Ranch."

He saw the telephone wires leading from the house. If I could just break in, he thought, and get Sally on that phone!

He turned Sunny into the corral, pitched him hay, then opened the box that contained axes, picks, and other equipment kept ready for forest-fire emergencies. He selected an ax and jammed it under the boards on a window, ignoring the signs posted everywhere, "U.S. Government Property. Keep off!"

Ten minutes later he was standing in the darkened house, lighting a match to find the number of the Marvin ranch. "Four longs and four shorts." He grabbed the handle and started ringing.

It was Sally who answered. Andy found himself jumbling up the story as he told it. "And then they took the horses—that is, after the bear had made old Eighteen buck Uncle Wes into the creek—"

"Take it easy, Andy." Sally's voice sounded far off and tinny. "I don't get it."

"O.K.," Andy said wearily. "I'll try again."

Sally kept at him until she had the whole thing clear

in her mind. "Atta boy, Andy," she said. "Don't you worry. I'll get the sheriff, and the deputies. We'll look after everything."

"O.K., Sally—and oh, yes, that plane." He gave the license number. "Uncle Wes said to be sure to tell you that."

"It's going to take a day, probably, to get in there, Andy." Sally said. "What are you going to do now?"

"Climb into the ranger's bed and sleep till doomsday," he yawned.

It was late afternoon when he awoke. He peered between cracks of the boarded-up window by his bed and saw that the weather had not changed. He lolled back between the soft sheets, feeling warm and lazy. Sunny had plenty of feed and water in the corral. Nothing to worry about there. They'd done their job. The rest was up to the sheriff. Pretty soon, if he didn't fall asleep again, he'd get up, light the stove, and dig into those groceries he'd seen in the kitchen. He'd start with tomato juice, he thought, a couple of eggs, some store bread. Gee, he was hungry.

But he didn't move. It was too warm and soft. Not like a bedroll.

Suddenly, he had a picture of Uncle Wes lying in the doorway on an old tarp with a gun in his hand. No soft bed for him!

Andy sat up. What was he doing here in the lap of luxury, when his uncle might—might be even fighting for his life? And Sally had said it might take a day to round up a posse.

Andy jumped out of bed and into his still-damp clothing. He'd have to rustle some grub and get back there fast.

As Andy approached the divide again that evening he was wondering what the United States government would do when they caught up with him. He had broken into government property, slept in the ranger's bed, eaten his food until he was ready to burst. Now he was equipped with some of the same ranger's thickest woolen socks—too large but warm—a good saddle slicker, a bridle for Sunny, one pocketful of oats to keep Sunny close to him, and another filled with sliced ham and a hunk of bread.

True, he had left a note for the ranger explaining everything and he hoped the government official would understand. After all, he was trying to help the government preserve the game, wasn't he? And a man had to be warm and dry in order to do a good job.

He rode along under the snow glacier, watching a foggy cloud above him. Now and then a slice of it would slide along the canyon below; then a wisp would drift over the divide just ahead. At first it rather entertained him. Riding a horse through the clouds was kind of exciting, even though it was almost dark.

Then he began to wonder if fog lay along the trail

on the other side of the divide. If so, he might easily get lost.

You can count on a horse to take you home, but Sunny now had no idea where Andy wanted to go. He urged the pony into a trot.

As they hit the top they entered a swirling mist. Sunny, unable to find the trail, stopped of his own accord. Beads of water lay along his mane; the pommel of the saddle in front of Andy shone with wet, and the drifting fog laid damp fingers against his cheek.

The cloud had closed in behind, too. Andy felt as though he were sitting on a horse suspended in space. It gave him a queer sensation in his stomach.

"Now don't scare yourself," he thought. "You're perfectly safe here."

But was he? He had a feeling that something or someone was near. He listened to the wet silence. Was there some sound he couldn't quite detect? He looked at Sunny's ears. They were pricked forward, and his head was turned slightly to the left.

Then there *was* something. You couldn't fool Sunny. He thought he heard a pebble rolling downhill, a tiny pebble.

Was it his imagination? Andy tried holding his breath. Yes, there it was again—a rock chuck maybe?

Sunny was listening, too, no doubt about it. Andy sat there, trying to make himself push on into the fog, but what he really wanted to do was turn around and go back—get out of the clammy mist; get away from the unknown something that was stalking him.

Then he felt Sunny tense. His legs bunched. He wanted to run but didn't dare. Andy started to turn him.

"Get off that horse, bub," a voice said, so close that Andy's heart jumped into his throat.

13

The Telltale Bridle

~~~~~~~~~~~~~~~~~~~~~~~~~~~~~~~~~~

"WHAT—WHO ARE YOU?" ANDY GASPED THROUGH A tight throat.

"Don't run that horse, bub," the voice said with a Scandinavian accent, "or, by golly, I'll have to bore a hole through you. Go on. Get off that pony."

Andy dismounted, furious at himself for his mistake. Of course, when he didn't show up at Pass Creek they'd searched for him, tracked him to the divide, and posted a guard. And he had to go and walk right into the trap!

"Couldn't wait to help Uncle Wes, huh!" he thought bitterly. "A lot of help I'll be now!"

He felt hands searching him. Then he could hear Heinie going over his saddle looking for guns.

"O.K.," Heinie said at last. "I think you can get on now. I take the reins. You follow."

Andy decided to keep his mouth shut until he could figure out what to do. He could never make a break for it in the fog, and he had promised Uncle Wes not to put up a fight.

165

Andy decided to keep his mouth shut until he could figure out what to do.

He climbed on Sunny without the reins, and soon he was traveling through the mist, a prisoner.

They came out of the clouds a mile below the divide, and Heinie broke into a trot, yanking on Sunny's bit until Andy wanted to cry out. Sunny, however, as though resigned to his fate, trotted along obediently, and by midnight they reached Garland's camp in Lost Basin.

They dismounted at the corral, leaving Sunny with his reins wound around a hitching rail, and headed for the cook tent.

There were no lights in the tepees, although he could hear men talking in low voices, but a lantern shone through the dirty canvas of the big bell tent. As they approached, Andy took a hitch in his belt. He'd had time to think now. For once he'd follow his uncle's instructions to the letter. He'd play "the dumb kid."

Heinie pulled back a tent flap and pushed Andy in ahead of him. He felt a wave of heat against his face. There was the smell of cheap tobacco and stale sweat. Andy blinked in the light of the two-mantled gasoline lamp and tried to make out the tent's occupants.

First he noticed Garland, sitting on an upturned pannier, then, as his eyes became accustomed to the light, he saw the dude he thought was Big Joe, leaning back in the shadows on a canvas cot. Near him, on a tarp, was the tommygun.

"Look what I found," Heinie said. "Boggin' around in the fog."

167

Garland jumped to his feet, knocking over the pannier. "You!" he said, striding up to Andy. "Ain't I glad to get my hands on you. Where you been?"

"I was lost," Andy said.

"Lost, huh? Why I been lookin' all over for you. You been down in the South Fork, ain't cha?"

"South Fork of what?" Andy asked, trying to look as stupid as possible.

"Don't start none of that!" Garland growled. "You tell me exactly where you been or I'll tie you to a tree and chap you."

"I haven't been anywhere in particular."

"Doggone if I don't square things with you." Garland bunched his fist. "You drew a bead on me the other day. Now you're goin' to pay for it."

"Shut up and sit down." It was a cold voice from the shadows. Andy remembered the tone. He'd heard it while lying behind the ridge. An even more dangerous man than Randy Garland, he thought.

"Let me get it out of him, Joe," Randy said. "This kid's been in my hair all summer. Now he's got no uncle to protect him."

"Sit down!" The voice was still expressionless. Garland retrieved the pannier and sat.

Andy stood in the corner of the tent waiting. The man in the shadows seemed to be looking him over from top to toe, biding his time, like a spider watching a fly. Andy shifted from one foot to another uncomfortably and tried to look as sad and bedraggled as possible. "Gee! I'm awful tired," he whined. "Could I go somewhere and get some sleep?"

"Sure," Big Joe leaned forward out of the shadows so that his heavy face hit the light. "Sure, kid. In just a minute, we'll give you some food and a nice bedroll. But first we'd like to get a little dope on you. You say you were lost. How come?"

"Well, all that fog kind of came down on me and I just didn't know where I was."

"Well, that must have been just the other side of the divide, right?"

"I guess so," Andy said.

"How were things at the ranch?"

A trick question, huh? Andy scratched his ear. "There's no ranch up there, is there?" he asked.

"Well, if you were on the other side of the divide, you must have gone down to your ranch."

"I haven't been on any ranch since I left uncle's." Andy sat down wearily on the ground.

"Stand up," Joe's voice was suddenly hard. "Go on, get up!" His eyes, glowing like a cat's in the lamplight, seemed to bore right through Andy.

Stumbling over the long, droopy slicker, Andy got to his feet. "Gee," he said. "I thought you'd let me get some sleep."

"Tell me exactly where you've been in the last twenty-four hours. Now talk and stop acting dumb."

169

Andy tried out his carefully prepared story. "Well, Uncle Wes gave me a message for the ranger, so I took it to the ranger station."

"I see. What did the ranger say?"

"I didn't see him."

"What do you mean you didn't see him? You said you delivered the message." The words spat at him like bullets.

"There was a note on his door. Said he was fighting a fire in the North Fork." Andy hugged himself inwardly at the truth of his next words. "So I left a message for him."

Big Joe leaned back in the shadows. "Is there a fire in the North Fork, Randy?" he asked.

"Yeah, I think so." Randy spat at the stove. "But that kid's lying."

"I am not," Andy said.

"What did you do after you left the message?" Joe was at him again.

"Started back here," Andy said truthfully.

"Where did you find your horse?" The question took Andy by surprise.

"Why—up the trail," he said.

"He's been wandering around here for days without a bridle," Joe said. "Does he have one now, Heinie?"

"Sure. I was surprised. I have good look." Heinie was excited. "I saw it when I tied the horse up. It's the ranger's bridle, I think."

"So you *were* in the ranger's cabin!" Joe got up suddenly, grabbed Andy by his slicker and lifted him almost off the ground. "The ranger doesn't leave his bridle around to be stolen. You were inside. You used the phone. You hollered for help, didn't you?" He shook the slicker suddenly. Andy rattled inside it like a pea, but he didn't say anything.

"Go on, talk!" The man's face was close to Andy's. The fat jowls worked, the lips pouted. Andy saw the black hairs on the thick wrist close to his chin. The wind was going out of him. He felt himself stumbling on the slicker as the man shook him.

"Talk!" the man said.

Andy gritted his teeth and tried to pull the hand away from his throat, but he didn't speak.

"You phoned for help, didn't you?"

The hand was like a bar of iron. Suddenly it let up.

"You called the cops. That's all we need to know anyway," Joe said, and pushed Andy from him.

Andy staggered back against the wall, and waited. For a moment there was no sound in the tent. All eyes were on Big Joe, watching, waiting for him to make the next move.

Big Joe settled back on his cot, thinking. Suddenly, he leaned forward, his eyes shining in the lamplight. "I think I've got an idea," he said slowly. "Take off that vest you've got under your jacket."

Andy took off the warm vest Uncle Wes had given him, and struggled back into his coat and slicker.

171

"Give it here." Big Joe held out his hand. Andy gave him the vest, wondering what Big Joe wanted with it.

"Now, Garland," Joe said. "Tie his hands and take him to the mine. I've got an idea this'll fix Wes Marvin once and for all."

A few minutes later, they were riding across the open ridge that led to the mine. A rising storm rushed through the trees. Andy felt sleet mixed with hail whipping into his face and soaking his chest.

Clint led Sunny, jerking the reins from time to time, and behind him Garland flipped a rope's end at Sunny's tail. Yanked in front and slapped from behind, the little horse jumped and lagged in turn, and Andy, with his hands tied behind him, had a hard time keeping his balance.

Only one thing kept up his spirits. The message was out. Sooner or later the sheriff and Sally would arrive with help. A posse on horseback could weather this storm, but no plane could land until the ceiling rose and the earth was dry again.

But what was Big Joe going to do with that vest? Andy was still puzzling about this when they arrived at the mine. They pulled him from his horse. The rope was retied around his wrists, and these in turn were tied to his ankles, so that his feet were bent under him.

Andy saw the flashlight pick out the mine door. Garland drew back the big squared log that served as a giant bolt. Then Andy felt himself picked up bodily and thrown into the cave.

His head slammed against rock. Pain stabbed his brain in a blinding whirl of sparks. The door closed on creaky hinges and the bar slid into place. Then Andy lost consciousness.

14

Prisoners in the Lost Mine

~~~~~~~~~~~~~~~~~~~~~~~~~~~~~~~

ANDY TRIED TO PULL HIMSELF UP THROUGH DEEP layers of darkness. He was conscious of pain between his eyes. There were queer flashes of dreams—of trying to catch Sunny in the dark, of a bear reaching out and grabbing him by the neck. There were noises somewhere. He wanted to find out what they were, but when he tried to raise his head, he felt sick at his stomach.

Much later, when Andy awoke again, his bent legs were straining at the ropes, pulling on his aching wrists, but his headache had eased, and the consciousness of all that had happened to him came back in a flood. He remembered his capture, the cave, the thick wooden bolt. He wondered how long he had been unconscious, but there was no way of telling. It was pitch dark, and the sound of the storm, if it was still going on, was lost in the solid rock.

Andy lay quietly, trying to make his muscles relax, and it was some time before he noticed the sound.

Suddenly he knew he wasn't alone. Some animal or somebody—

"Who's that?" he shouted, his voice harsh and very loud in the cave. He heard the terror in it himself. He was helpless. There was something near. "Get away!" he shouted.

The thing moved. A tired, quiet voice said, "You awake, Andy? You all right?"

"Uncle Wes!" Andy gasped.

"Are you hurt, boy?"

"No," Andy sighed. "I've got a headache and I'm sore all over—but, Uncle Wes, what have they done to you? How'd you get here?"

"Well, they told me they found you on the trail with a broken leg and showed me the vest to prove it. Naturally, I had to find you."

"Gee, I wondered why Big Joe took that vest," Andy said. "But, Uncle Wes, are you hurt?"

"Just bruised up a bit. When I realized you were a prisoner, I put up a scrap, but it was too late, of course. Too many of 'em."

"How's the ankle?"

"Better. Anyway, it was the last time I had a chance to walk on it. I'm hog-tied tighter'n a calf."

"So am I." Andy knew it was all over now. They not only had him and all the horses, they'd even captured Uncle Wes himself. Big Joe, Garland—all of them—would fly away now, scot-free. "Gee," he said. "I guess we're washed up for sure this time, Uncle Wes."

Wes's voice answered in the darkness with a hardness

175

Andy had never heard before. "No, we're not," he said. "Not by a darn sight. Did you get the message out?"

"You bet I did!" Andy told him of all his adventures since he had left the cabin. So much had happened that it seemed weeks since he had waved to Uncle Wes leaning against the doorframe.

"That's great!" Uncle Wes said when Andy had finished. "You've done a first-rate job, Andy, and you've used your head all the way. I've been the stupid one. I fell into their trap. But I just had to find out what happened to you."

Uncle Wes's voice was bitter. Andy was glad he couldn't see his uncle trussed up and helpless. "I know, Uncle Wes," he said, sympathetically. "Gee, you weren't going to let 'em hurt me."

They were silent for a time and the stillness of the cave began to weigh on Andy. The air was heavy and musty-smelling, and he found himself listening, waiting for something to happen. Then he realized that nothing was going to change now. No water—tied hand and foot. It might be days before even Sally thought to look for them here. Andy began to shiver. A chill crept up his back. He felt himself sweating into his damp shirt, and the walls of the cave seemed to close in on him. "Uncle Wes," he said, and fear was in his voice. "What'll we do? If we stay here we may—"

"Take it easy, kid," Uncle Wes said. "Don't lose your nerve. Sooner or later Sally and the sheriff are bound to check this cave. They know the meat was kept here. They'll find we aren't on the job and they'll look for us and find us—if we're still here."

Andy was only half convinced. His fatigue was eating into him. His thoughts raced in circles, like scared horses running around a corral trying to find a way out. "But what can we do?" he said, trying not to feel the heavy walls around him.

"We've got to think that out," Uncle Wes said. "Sally and the sheriff must be on their way. Now we've got to figure out what our enemies are up to."

Uncle Wes went on talking quietly. Andy knew that his uncle was trying to calm him, to turn his mind from fear. The voice was soothing, and Andy found himself listening, forgetting to be scared, even becoming hopeful.

"You see, Andy," Wes was saying, "Garland is a bad hombre, but he's scared. He knows we've got enough on him now to put him in the old hoosegow. We might even get him on a kidnaping charge. But from what you tell me, I'd say he was taking his orders from that Big Joe buzzard, and even Big Joe must be frightened. He knows a posse's after him. If his plane doesn't show up before the posse gets here, he's in for a fight—and he'll take a licking."

"But it will show up, Uncle Wes, as soon as the clouds lift."

"Well, the weather's been on our side anyway," Uncle Wes answered. "When I got here the storm had let up, but there was snow on the ground. Don't think a plane could land until the ground's dry. It's pretty mucky out there now. Say, have you seen my hat?"

Andy was surprised at the sudden change in the conversation. Why did Uncle Wes want his hat, of all things? "No, Uncle Wes. I can't see anything."

Uncle Wes laughed. "That's true. It was a silly question, but roll around a bit and see if you can connect with it."

Andy thought his uncle was just trying to keep his mind occupied, but he began rocking his body around the floor of the cave, feeling for something squashy and soft that might be made of felt.

His uncle thumped about in the dark, too. Andy didn't understand, but he kept searching.

"Here it is," Wes said finally. "I thought I remembered 'em throwing it in before they closed the door." His voice was thick, and Andy realized that Wes had the brim of the hat in his teeth.

"Gee, Uncle Wes," Andy said. "What good will your hat do?"

"You'll see," Wes said, "if it works! Now near my head are what seem to be shavings or bits of wood. Do you remember seeing any more of 'em, Andy, when you were here before?"

"Sure." Andy was puzzled. "There's a lot of stuff brushed up against the wall over there. Garland hacked out some braces to hold up the old mine timbers."

"Good! Now here's what you do, Andy. Wiggle over

to the wall and push along some of those shavings. Shove with your head or your chin. Take your time, but push 'em along until you get to me."

Andy thumped slowly across to the wall, inching like a measuring worm, until he felt his head hit the side of the cave. He could hear his uncle moving a few feet away. He, too, seemed to be collecting rubbish.

Andy felt with his tongue until he had located some of the rubble, then started pushing it with his head to where he thought his uncle lay.

It was a desperately slow and painful job. Andy knew there must be some sense to it, but he avoided asking further questions. He felt his cheek grow raw as he shoved the rubbish along the floor. He tried to use the back of his head instead, but this twisted his legs and wrists in the rope, increasing the pain unbearably.

Finally, he felt his head bump his uncle's knee. Wes had pushed himself by main strength up the side of the wall.

"I'm sitting on my legs, Andy," he said. "My head's against the wall and my wrists are behind me. Push that rubble under 'em. You'll find a lot of stuff there already. Pile it up as high as you can."

Andy pushed with his cheek, his ear, and even his tongue, until he felt the pile rise under Wes's wrists. He felt along the wrist and suddenly understood.

"A match, Uncle Wes! You've got a match!" he said.

"Yeah, found two in my hatband," Uncle Wes

179

answered. "They're kind of damp, but it wasn't actually raining when I got here. They may work." Wes kept a few matches in his Stetson, Andy remembered, because they were easier to get at than his pockets when wearing chaps.

"Are you going to burn the ropes? Won't your wrists burn, too?"

"Probably," Wes said. "Watch, and we'll see."

Andy lay with his face a foot or two from the little pile of rubble, rubbing his sore tongue against his teeth where the splinters had pricked the tender flesh.

He heard his uncle shuffling against the wall, trying to reach with the match and connect with the rock.

There was a sudden spurt, a tiny blue flare that looked twice its natural size in the dark. It fizzled for a moment, then caught the wood of the match. Uncle Wes waited until the flame was a clear triangle of yellow, then dropped it on the pile of rubbish.

While it burned, Andy felt himself struggling with it, trying by sheer will power to make it light the shavings below. There was a sudden pungent odor of pine smoke. Then the match went out.

"Shuffle up that pile a little, Andy," Wes said. "Try to get the small stuff on top."

Wearily, Andy worked on the pile with his teeth, trying to get light shavings on top. He knew it was the last chance, the single try left for freedom.

"O.K.," he said at last. "After you get it lit, lower

the match a bit, Uncle Wes. The stuff's piled higher against the wall and you'll be able to get the flame under it. When she starts, I'll blow on it."

"Good boy! Get set."

This time Andy stayed closer to Wes's elbow and kept his face to the floor, trying to point his mouth to where he had seen the flame. He knew that there would be one second when blowing might help. If he blew too hard, it might go out, but if he did it just right, when one or two shavings had caught, he might help ignite the rest of them.

Andy waited, hardly daring to breathe at all. His uncle seemed terribly deliberate. He was taking no chances of pushing over the pile or of letting the matchstick break. Andy wondered how he could feel what he was doing. His own hands had long ago gone completely numb.

There it was! The scratch, the spitting sound, the blue flare, and then, once again, a cone of yellow.

Uncle Wes held the tiny burning stick for what seemed hours. Andy was afraid that the numb hand was unable to let go. But finally the match dropped, not so far this time, and hit the shavings piled high against the wall.

The flame faded. Andy felt his life, his entire existence, dying with a match end.

Then there was a sputter. A single shaving caught and flared, showing a bit of rope and an inch of skin. Another shaving caught.

181

Andy blew softly. A small stick, more substantial than a shaving, began to burn. Andy puffed little spurts of breath against the pile. It caught, glowing red within, and flames, real substantial flames, began to lick at Wes's wrists.

"Move your wrists a little to the right," Andy said, "and pull on them like crazy, Uncle Wes."

Uncle Wes didn't answer, but he moved his hands so that the greatest peak of flame burned against the rope between his hands.

Andy watched the flames lick at the hemp and flesh. The smoke was thickening. He heard his uncle cough and his breath came fast. Andy could hear the pain in it. But Uncle Wes said nothing.

The flames were higher now, too high, Andy thought. They licked at Wes's arms. The cave itself suddenly came to life with shadows flicking in the corners, and a dull orange glow struck the beams along the roof.

Andy found himself gritting his teeth, trying to share his uncle's pain. He could see the muscles, taut along the glowing arms, pulling on the rope. The kneeling figure with wild hair and glowing eyes was like some strange Indian priest burning a sacrifice before a hidden shrine.

Andy thought he smelled burning flesh through the pungent odor of pine. "Uncle Wes!" he yelled. "You're —you're burning."

Suddenly he saw his uncle's arms tense in a great

effort. Wes gasped, pulled, tore at the rope. Then he fell forward on his face.

Andy rolled toward him, crying, "Uncle Wes! You all right?"

Wes gasped. "Put that fire out. We need the air!" Andy rolled on the fire, trying to smother it. He heard Wes coughing. Then suddenly two strong hands picked him clear of the fire.

"O.K., kid," he said. "I've got it now."

Wes was on his feet shaking off the ropes, with queer fumbling movements of his numb hands. Then he stamped out the remaining fire.

"Nice going," he said. Andy felt his own wrists loosened, and a few minutes later they were chafing their numb limbs and grinning at each other in the dark.

"Sorry to make you roll on that fire. That was dangerous," Uncle Wes said. "But I was afraid I was going to pass out there for a moment and there's a lot of dry wood here. I wanted to make sure we didn't choke to death."

Andy felt the blood begin to circulate in his hands. He worked his fingers, wiggled his toes, and finally stretched and walked about the cave, enjoying the freedom of movement. His spirits were soaring again. "What would you like to eat, Uncle Wes?" he asked.

"A venison steak, a pile of French fries, a mug of hot coffee, and a couple of double-dip ice-cream cones for dessert," Uncle Wes said ruefully.

"Well, I can't deliver that," Andy said, reaching into

183

his pockets, "but I've got two slices of ham, kinda battered, but still good. Some bread, too."

The bread was crumbling and damp, the ham tasted like bits of rawhide, but the two of them ate ravenously as though it was the finest food on earth.

15

Uncle Wes Ropes a Dude

〜〜〜〜〜〜〜〜〜〜〜〜〜〜〜〜〜〜〜〜〜〜〜

*N*ow, ANDY, YOU WERE IN HERE WITH THE DOOR open," Uncle Wes said when they had finished eating. "What can you remember about it?"

"That door's thick, Uncle Wes, and brand-new," Andy said. "And the crossbar is as big as a two-by-four. I can't see any way to break it down."

"How about the doorframe? Is that new, too?"

Andy thought awhile. No, he didn't think so. They had simply slung the door to the old mine entrance timbers.

Uncle Wes found the entrance, tried to shove the door open with his shoulder, then began prodding the frame with his jackknife, a big one he used for cleaning fish and skinning game.

"The frame's punky, Andy," he said. "The centers of the logs are sound, but the rest is rotten." He explained to Andy what he was trying to do. First he ran the blade up and down the crack between the door and the frame, until he had located the place where the crossbar lay. Then he began cutting away the frame around it.

185

Andy unclasped his stubby jackknife and went to work below. For a long time neither of them spoke. The only sound was the picking of the knives as they dug through the wood, like mice gnawing under a floor at home, Andy thought.

He felt blisters rising on his fingers, and bits of wood from his uncle's knife dropped onto his head.

The hard core of timber resisted stubbornly. Andy had stopped to rest, when he heard his uncle grunt. A tiny hole of light had appeared, showing his uncle's unshaven face, a pale mask in the gloom.

"Door overlaps some places," Wes said, without stopping his whittling. "Got to dig through a bit of that, too."

Andy went back to work, but the stubby blade was inefficient. He found himself resting more frequently, while his uncle scraped on without pause, gnawing their way toward freedom. His eyes were intense, his body hunched, and Andy could feel the anger that drove him on. He was mighty glad that he was on his uncle's side, he thought. He would hate to be Randy Garland if Uncle Wes ever met him on even terms again.

Andy rested his back to the door, trying to whip up enough energy to go on digging. He fell asleep just as he was, his knife open in his hand.

The light faded from the widening crack as another night came on, and even Wes paused from time to time, unclenching his fingers, limbering up his hands for further work. There was a whirling sound of wind from the outside, and, as the crack grew larger, a few tiny particles of snow sifted through the slit. Wes licked them from the wood, savoring the few drops of water with his tongue, then went on digging.

"Andy! Wake up now. I need you."

Andy's eyes opened on semidarkness. A tiny patch of flickering light drifted through the oval hole that Wes had dug through the doorframe and around the log that barred the entrance. Andy couldn't tell how long he had slept, except by the size of the hole. It must have been many hours. His hand still held the knife, and he closed the blade stiffly.

"Gee," he said, "you've sure worked hard, Uncle Wes."

"Shhh," Wes whispered, "that's firelight coming through the crack. There's a guard outside."

"What do we do now?" Andy rose and stretched his cramped limbs.

"Your fingers are smaller than mine," Wes answered. "Slip 'em through that hole and see if you can get a grip on the bar. Try and slide it back."

Andy's fingers crept into the hole, feeling for the underside of the squared log. He found it, cold and hard along his nails, and managed to get two fingers under it. He pushed upward as hard as he could and felt it move.

"Dig sideways a little more, Uncle Wes," he said, withdrawing his fingers. "I can lift it up, but I haven't room to slide it along."

187

Uncle Wes dug awhile; then Andy tried again. Now with more room, the bar began to slide a fraction of an inch at a time. Andy remembered that only a heavy wooden brace held it to the door. That meant it had to fit loosely. He worked until his fingers numbed.

Suddenly there was a cracking sound from the door. Andy withdrew his fingers. "She's open," he whispered triumphantly. "We're free!"

Uncle Wes stood behind him, coiling a rope. "Don't open it yet," he said. "We'll have to do it slowly. The hinges are cold, and it's going to crack like a pistol volley."

Andy stepped away from the door and waited. Uncle Wes, the rope coiled in his right hand, began to push the door open a few inches at a time. Whenever a whirl of wind whistled through the trees, he shoved it further, blending the sound with the creaking of tree branches outside.

Andy found he was holding his breath, watching freedom appear by inches, as trees, brambles, and the flickering glint of firelight gradually came into view. A swirl of wet snow blew suddenly in the doorway, and Andy drew deep breaths of stormy air.

Uncle Wes beckoned to him, and he followed through the door.

Outside, the mask of brambles concealing the entrance was covered with a film of glistening ice that sparkled in the firelight. Through them, Andy could see the little fire in the glade. A man, one of the dudes, Andy thought, sat hunched near the embers, his collar high around his neck, his new Stetson brittle with ice. From time to time he shifted his feet to the fire, and once he blew his nose and coughed, as though catching a cold.

Uncle Wes, with Andy following, crept over a half inch of snow that deadened sound. As Wes turned to whisper to him, Andy saw the copper glint of his eyes in the firelight, the grim mouth that was almost smiling, and the fingers on the rope shaking out a loop in the snow.

Andy grinned at his uncle to show how happy he was. This was the real thing. This was attack!

Wes whispered so close to his ear that he could feel the breath in it. "When I say 'go,' dive for his legs."

Then Wes stepped into the circle of firelight, dragging the loop behind him. "Hey!" he shouted.

The man in the frozen Stetson jumped to his feet. Andy recognized the ratty little figure as one of Big Joe's gang. He was fumbling under his clumsy coat for a pistol.

At that second, Wes flicked his arm. There was no whirling the rope around his head. He struck like a snake. His arm, swinging overhand with the California twist, lashed out; the loop dropped over the Stetson, around the arms, and yanked tight.

"Go," Wes snapped.

Andy ran low at the staggering little man. He tore at the legs as he would at the football dummy at school.

189

He hit them a fraction below the knees and the man crashed into the snow, trying to kick free.

Andy hung on grimly, while Wes worked up the rope, keeping it taut. He trussed the man up like a sack of meal, took his gun, and dragged him into the cave. Andy was almost sorry for the dude. He never seemed to know what struck him. He whimpered once or twice like a puppy, but the door closed on him, and the bar slid to. Wes jammed it into place with some sticks to wedge it tight, then hobbled back to the fire.

"Throw on some wood, Andy," he said, cheerfully. "Let 'em know that their guard's awake."

Andy built up the blaze and looked at his uncle testing his bad leg. "Your ankle sure is better," he said.

"Uh-huh." Wes's face was thoughtful as he gazed at the flames. "Weak, though. Can't count on it for any speed. Let's reconnoiter."

He led Andy down through the woods until they reached the meadows that surrounded Garland's camp. They dropped to their hands and knees and crawled up behind a log. When they peered over it all they could see was an expanse of white with some dark figures on it and, off to the right, the tiny glow of a fire.

"Have to wait for dawn to see anything," Wes said, and then lay quiet, his battered old hat over his eyes.

Andy, having left his cumbersome slicker in the cave, felt the snow seeping through his windbreaker. His hands and feet went numb again, and he moved around restlessly, waiting for dawn. He wondered how Wes could be still hour after hour, as though it were perfectly normal to lie on your back in the snow with your head on a rotten log.

Dawn came imperceptibly. The cloud ceiling was still low, but the wind had dropped and only a flake or two of snow drifted down.

Gradually, the near-by bushes sheathed in ice came into view, then more distant trees, and, finally, the base of the ridge behind them.

Andy turned and gazed over the log.

He saw a bunch of grazing horses. Near them, on the palomino, Clint's stiff figure, his collar around his ears, was silhouetted against the snow. Off to the right was the fire, now little more than a smudge of smoke against the dawn light. Still farther off, Andy could just see the tents of Garland's camp.

He heard a dry chuckle next to him. "Ridin' night herd on their cavvy," Wes said, softly. "They want to be able to get away fast."

Andy thought it over. The sheriff hadn't arrived, but neither had the plane. They were waiting out there, ready to break for the hills, but if the ceiling lifted, and it looked as though it might, the plane would be in.

"You know what?" The hardness had left Wes's face. He looked like a grizzled small boy with mischief in his smile. "I'd sure like to see that bunch of dudes afoot in this weather."

191

Clint's stiff figure on the palomino was silhouetted against
the snow.

"So would I," Andy said. "If only that Clint would go in and eat, I could run out and stampede 'em."

"Maybe."

Andy could identify the other horses now, and he saw with a sudden wave of excitement that the nearest one, grazing just a few feet from the others, was Sunny.

They had pulled off his saddle and bridle, and he was trying to graze with the rest of the bunch, but, like any new horse, he was an outcast to the community. Every few minutes, with fearsome snorts, one of the geldings would turn on him and chase him away.

Sunny would run a few feet, swap ends, and snap out both hind feet in vicious kicks, laying his ears back and waving his head in fury. Then the gelding would return to the herd, and Sunny would start to move in again.

Andy watched Sunny's flashing speed, his incredible quickness. He wanted to get his arms around that warm neck, to feel the soft nose in his hand, and to slide on that short back—and—and—

"Uncle Wes," he whispered. "I think I could catch Sunny!"

Wes shook his head. "Not a chance," he said.

"Did it before," Andy said excitedly. "Caught him on the trail in the middle of the night."

"Not from a bunch, you didn't."

"Let me try, Uncle Wes. Give me a chance."

"Well," Uncle Wes looked dubious. "It's a pretty long shot, Andy. How in blazes do you expect to walk into a herd and make your horse come out? You can't rope him afoot in the open."

"I can't rope anywhere," Andy said. "I'll use oats."

"O.K.," Wes said. "You can have a try when Clint goes in to breakfast."

Andy reached into his pockets for the oats he had saved for emergencies. He hunted through every seam. But the last few grains, pulled out with the food or lost while rolling around in the cave, were gone. Andy felt his hopes dwindling. Sunny would never leave the bunch for nothing. He explained to his uncle about the oats. "I'm pretty sure he won't come without 'em," he groaned.

"Well, try it anyway," Uncle Wes said. "Take your time. If the little horse loves you as much as you think, he just *might* come. Besides," he went on, "we're doing no good here, and sooner or later they'll discover us."

Wes reached under his coat and unwrapped the remainder of the burned rope that had trussed him up. "I never waste rope," he grinned. "Most always it turns out to be useful."

Just then, while it was still early dawn, Clint rode around the herd. He bunched them together and drove Sunny, kicking and bucking, in among them. Then he turned away and rode toward the distant fire.

Wes made a honda and a loop from the rope and gave it to Andy. "Now," he said.

Andy crawled into the snow.

194

16

Andy and Sunny Strike Back

~~~~~~

A NDY FOUND HIMSELF BEHIND A SLIGHT RISE OF ground and made the most of the cover. Lying flat, he decided he could not be observed from the distant fire, although, if Clint started back, he would see the wiggly little trail left by Andy's body in the snow.

He reached the top and waited. The cavvy was still milling around, and it took some time for it to spread out again.

Andy heard snorts and squeals from the center, then Sunny came flying out, weaving his neck, his heels flying. But he was on the wrong side of the bunch. There was nothing to do but watch and hope.

He raised his head and looked at the campfire. Clint's horse, the palomino, was standing with his reins down, and Clint was drinking hot coffee, his back to the cavvy.

He turned to watch Sunny again. The horse was circling the bunch, trying to find a way to get in among them. Slowly, he approached Andy's side of the bunch, grazing a little, pretending that he had no intention of closing in, but gradually moving nearer.

195

Andy went up on his elbows. "Sunny!" he called, just above a whisper.

It was enough to carry to those sensitive mustang ears. Sunny jumped, spun on his heels, and faced the sound, his head up, ears forward, frosty breath snorting surprise.

Other horses looked up, too. It wouldn't do to excite the whole herd, Andy thought. It might bring Clint back. He waited awhile, but so did Sunny, standing like a little golden statue against the white of the snow. Andy admired every curve of him, and particularly the alert way he held his head and ears. Boy, that pony was sure a live one!

"Sunny," he called again in the same low voice. "Sunny! Come!"

Sunny quivered all over. He advanced a few steps, picking his front feet high off the ground, snorting steam. It was cold. He felt good. And that sure sounded like the boss's voice. Did it come from that queer lump huddled in the snow?

Andy called again, using words that Sunny knew, telling him lies he hated to tell. "Oats," he called, softly. "Carrots!" He wished he had some grains to crackle; that had worked last time. But now he had nothing. It was cold and Sunny was spooky. Andy held his hand out slowly in front of him as though he had oats.

Sunny looked back at the other horses. Should he leave them for the boss, if it *was* the boss? Andy thought -

196

Boy, that pony was sure a live one!

he could read the indecision in the horse's mind. He called again.

Curiosity mastered Sunny. He began to walk forward, his head close to the ground, still blowing steam, trying to make sure of the scent of his master in the snowy air.

As the horse approached, Andy, still on his hands and knees, started backing away toward the trees.

Then a mare in the bunch nickered. Sunny stopped and looked around. After all, maybe he was safer out in the open with the others. He turned and trotted back to the bunch.

Andy stifled a cry of disappointment and lay flat again.

As Sunny reached the bunch, the same gelding Andy had seen before rushed out and tore at Sunny with his mouth open, his teeth driving for Sunny's neck. Sunny spun round, kicked and galloped away again, shaking his golden mane.

"Sunny!" Andy called again.

Sunny stopped, hesitated, then turned his head and sent a last whinny toward the grazing horses, as if to say, "Phooy on you guys. This sure *is* the boss. And I'm going with *him!*" As Andy started scuttling like a crab back toward the trees, Sunny followed, his mind made up at last.

When they reached the trees, Andy rose up slowly to a standing position, and Sunny walked right up to him, throwing out his muzzle for the expected oats.

Andy slipped the rope around his neck and led him to the log where Wes' was lying.

"That's the darnedest exhibition of horse catching I've ever seen," Wes said, shaking his head unbelievingly. "You shinny out there like a snake, and your horse follows you back. That pony sure loves you."

Andy was hugging Sunny's neck. "I guess he does at that," he said, trying not to seem too proud.

"Now," Wes said. "How are you at riding Injun—bareback with a rope halter?"

"I've practiced on Sunny quite a lot," Andy said. "He's used to it."

"O.K.," Wes said. "How long do you think it would take you to skirt this meadow, keeping out of sight in the woods until you are just about opposite where we are now?"

Andy looked at the meadow stretching away to the south to where the trees bounded it.

"A good hour, maybe an hour and a half," he said.

"Take an hour and a half. Keep out of sight, and don't let that little horse's golden coat show where Clint can see him. If he misses Sunny he may start trailing you."

"What do I do when I reach the other side?" Andy asked. But he thought he knew, and the excitement rose in him. Uncle Wes was in the groove. He was having ideas!

Wes scratched his stubbly chin. "Wait," he said. "I'm going up to the sentinel rock we watched from the other day. I'll have to crawl most of the way. But I don't think they'll post a guard there. It's out of the

199

way. When you hear me let loose with that dude's popgun, Garland's boys will all be after me. Then you ride out and see if you can stampede those ponies. If you succeed, give the old Powder River cowboy yell and get those ponies over the ridge."

"O.K. Where'll I pick you up?"

"On the butte behind our cabin. I'll fade into the woods and show up there sooner or later. The farther they trail me from their landing field, the longer it'll take 'em to get back to it."

As he led Sunny through the trees, Andy's step was light, and every once in a while he turned to feast his eyes on the sorrel behind him.

"We're free again, Sunny, old man," he said gleefully. "And this time we'll put a scare into *them* for a change."

Sunny pushed Andy with his nose to remind him of the carrots that were owed him and almost knocked Andy over a deadfall.

It was noon when, still well hidden in the trees, he reached the opposite side of the meadow. He kept his hand on Sunny's nose. It wouldn't do to have him whinny at the horses out there.

He crept up as near as he dared to the edge of the grass and made a hackamore around Sunny's head, doubling back the rope so that he had something to neck-rein with. Then there was nothing to do but wait.

Over two hours had passed when Andy began to get nervous. What had happened to Uncle Wes? Had he walked into a guard, with only that dude pistol to protect him?

Andy looked at the ridge. He could see the sentinel rock, standing like some old chimney from a burned-out house. There was an open section of ridge across from him. If he could get the cavvy across it, that would bring him close to his uncle, he thought. There were game trails all along there, where elk came down for water. It shouldn't be too hard.

The Garland cavvy was drifting up the valley now, but they were well bunched, and Clint didn't seem to be worried. He was lying down, taking a nap after his long night vigil, and his horse, the reins trailing, cropped the grass near by.

Andy fidgeted. The tension kept mounting in him. He began to think of all the things that could happen. Uncle Wes might be a prisoner again, or Clint might easily overtake Sunny on the big palomino before he could drive the horses away, or Clint might grab the rifle from his saddle and start shooting—and he might hit Sunny!

The trees dripped around him. The snow was melting, and already only a patch or two remained in the meadow. That was good, Andy thought, nervously. That meant it would be harder to trail him.

For the hundredth time, Andy looked through the trees, plotting just where to run Sunny so that he could keep from being swept from the horse's back. It had

201

to come soon! But suppose nothing happened. Suppose Uncle Wes never did—

His thoughts were interrupted by a shot.

From the top of the ridge, Andy heard what sounded like a dozen madmen shouting, "There they are!" "Cut 'em down." More shots. "Powder River!"

Andy made a flying leap for Sunny's back. Surprised, Sunny jumped forward and Andy found himself lying across the horse's back, his legs dangling, his belly on the horse's backbone, his head hanging over. He reached out his hand, grabbed Sunny's mane, and, swinging his leg over, pulled himself into position.

As they burst into the meadow, Andy looked over his shoulder at Clint. The man's eyes were glued to a pair of binoculars trained on the sentinel rock. The palomino stood invitingly with his reins down. It was taking a chance! A risk! But if he could stampede that palomino, too—

Andy turned Sunny directly toward the campfire and kicked him harder than he'd ever been kicked before.

The palomino looked up at the sound of thundering hoofs. He saw an orange flash ridden by a wild figure swinging a rope's end coming at him with the speed of a locomotive. He took off, swinging his head expertly so as not to step on his reins, and ran toward his friends in the cavvy.

Andy and Sunny rocketed after him, racing across the soft meadow until they had closed in. The palomino was having trouble with the dangling reins, and Andy

202

saw Clint's gun sticking from the saddle scabbard. He looked back over his shoulder and grinned at the figure running after him. "Powder River," he yelled, signaling Uncle Wes that all was well. "It's a mile wide, an inch deep and it flows uphill from Texas! Powder River. Let 'er buck!"

He heard shots over the sound of hoofs, and wondered if his uncle had answered with, "Too thick to drink, too thin to plow! Powder River!"

By this time, they were approaching the rest of the cavvy, and they, too, began to run, bucking and snorting with surprise.

Sunny herded the palomino in with the others and turned them toward the ridge.

Andy looked behind him again and saw men running toward Clint, who was yelling and shaking his fist. Finally, someone, Garland perhaps, raised a rifle and took a long shot at Andy. But Andy was a small target now, a mere blob on a streak of orange. He saw the bullet spit into the mud at least fifty yards behind him.

As the horses approached the ridge, they slowed down and tried to turn from the band of timber at the base of it, but under Andy's guidance Sunny kept after them, and they plowed in among the trees, following Garland's big bay.

Sunny was blowing, and Andy began to feel the letdown. His knees ached from gripping Sunny's ribs; his hand seemed frozen in the horse's mane. But he was busy planning. Obviously, Uncle Wes had been success-

203

ful. He'd fade back now into the aspen grove, working down toward Big Game Creek.

When the cavvy reached the top of the ridge a mile above the chimney boulder, the horses stopped and looked back, blowing heavily.

Andy pushed Sunny as hard as he dared. This was no time for the bunch to break up. Garland would be after them, might even catch them if they got wound up in the timber.

When he reached the top, he gave Sunny no chance to breathe, but drove him into the herd and sent it plunging along the sidehill behind the ridge. He was aiming for the bottom of the aspen grove, but the going was rough. The horses stumbled. They kept trying to spread out, and Sunny, his neck a lather of sweat, plunged up and down the rough sage-covered ground to keep them in line.

The palomino, in spite of his skill, kept stepping on his reins and yanking the bit in his mouth. It slowed him up until Sunny loped up to him and waited for Andy to turn loose with the rope's end.

But Andy had another idea. Here was a chance to catch a horse, all saddled and bridled, for Uncle Wes. He eased Sunny up alongside and reached for the palomino's reins. He was above, reaching down, and he loosened his knees to lean further.

He could see the palomino's eye showing white with alarm, and there were flecks of blood in the foam around the horse's mouth where the bit had cut him.

It would have been easy if Andy had been in a saddle. He reached further; his fingertips reached the palomino's rein and got a good grip. He tightened his hand just as the horse jumped sideways.

Desperately, Andy tried to regain his balance. Sunny, feeling his master's weight uneven on his back, slowed down, but Andy kept on going.

His body slashed into the sagebrush. The breath slammed out of him. His belly raked the rough ground, rocks and sage tore at his cheeks, but instinctively he clung to the palomino's reins.

He came to a few seconds later, lying on the sidehill, gasping like a fish out of water. The scenery gradually stopped spinning around him in pinwheels of light, his vision steadied, and he saw the palomino standing above him, his eyes wild, ready to pull away from the strange panting thing in front of him.

Andy sat up and looked around. A few feet away, Sunny stood with his ears forward, the rope halter pulled drunkenly over one of them. His look of wild surprise said, plainly, "Left kind of suddenly, didn't you, boss?"

As his wind came back, Andy stood up gingerly. More scratches, more bruises, but no bones broken, he decided. He looked at the cavvy spreading out into the aspen grove and down the hill. No time to waste. "Come on, Pal, old boy," he said.

17

Big Joe Starts Closing In

〜〜〜〜〜〜〜〜〜〜〜〜〜〜〜〜〜〜〜〜〜〜〜

*A*NDY SLID UP ON SUNNY AND, LEADING THE PALO-
mino, began rounding up the horses again and driving
them toward the bottom of the aspen grove and the
Big Game Creek trail. As they passed below where Andy
thought the sentinel rock stood, he risked a yell. If the
enemy wasn't too close, Uncle Wes might answer.

"Powder River!" he yelled.

"Let 'er buck," came the answer immediately.

Andy looked up the ridge and saw Wes stumbling
toward him waving a pistol in each hand. "Want to buy
a good saddle horse?" Andy yelled.

"You bet," Uncle Wes came puffing up, sticking the
two automatics in his belt. "Good boy, Andy. I can
sure use that pony."

"I'll throw in a good rifle, Uncle Wes," Andy said,
pointing to the saddle scabbard. He laughed at the light
in his uncle's eyes. He could see Wes had been success-
ful; he was enjoying himself.

Uncle Wes climbed stiffly into the saddle, easing his
sore right leg into the stirrup. "Fits pretty good," he

said. "Let's go. Drive 'em to the cabin first ano pick up some supplies. Those bums are after us with every-thing short of a bazooka."

For two hours they worked like beavers. They drove the Garland horses into the cabin corral, picked out two pack ponies and packed them with a bedroll, food, ammunition, and several bottles of water.

Next, Andy shortened the stirrups on the palomino's saddle and transferred it to Sunny. It was too large, but easier than riding bareback. Wes transferred his own saddle to Pal.

Finally, they retrieved their rifles, some extra clothes, and the field glasses, and, driving the Garland string before them, rode up the butte behind the cabin.

When they reached the top, Andy saw why Uncle Wes had picked it as the best place to withstand a possible siege. Crumbling boulders of pudding stone lay about the bald top of the ridge, affording ample protection. Anyone attacking them would have to cross a hundred yards of steep, open sidehill, no matter from which direction he approached. And if the plane arrived while they were here, they would have a good two hours of walking to get to it.

They drove the pack horses in among the rocks and unpacked them, while the remainder of the bunch grazed around the edges, too tired to wander.

Andy slipped the bedroll into a cranny between two boulders and unpacked the food panniers, while Uncle Wes rewrapped his tired ankle.

"Where did you get that second pistol, Uncle Wes?" Andy asked.

"Well," Wes pulled the little .38 from his pocket. "This pepper pot came from another of those dudes. He was sittin' by the old sentinel rock when I got there, wishing he was back in the city where he could keep warm. I crawled up and jumped on him."

"Much of a fight?"

"Nope. Not much. I tied his hands. And when I was ready I said, 'Yell, Mister!' He yelled."

"So that's why it sounded as though there were a lot of guys up there!" Andy said. "I couldn't see how one man could make so much noise. Where is he now?"

"Oh, I turned him loose with his hands tied. Told him every sheriff in Wyoming was on the way here. Had no way to take him with me."

"I'll bet he's telling Big Joe all about it by now."

"Yep. But Big Joe won't scare. Unless I miss my guess, he'll be madder'n a bull in fly time."

"Do you think he'll attack us here?" Andy asked.

"Maybe." Wes pulled his boot on. "But not right away. He's got to find us first. And remember they're all afoot. I just hope he'll come looking for us. It'll take him that much further away from his landing field, and Sally and the sheriff are bound to be here by morning."

Andy wasn't sure that Uncle Wes himself believed that last statement. Maybe he thought something had happened to Sally. She should have been here long ago, Andy thought.

Big Joe Starts Closing In

Wes tried to hide the worried look behind his eyes. "Now, Andy," he said, "you've got to hold the fort while I hide this pack string."

Andy felt his heart sink. He didn't feel much like waiting here alone. It was all very well with his uncle around, but lying up here by himself with a dozen guys armed to the teeth looking for him was something else.

"Can't help it," Wes said. "I won't be gone long." He pointed down the far side of the butte to what looked like unbroken forest. "About five miles into that stuff there's a park with good grass," he went on. "If I can put those ponies in there, they'll stay until they've filled up, and even if they drift back it'll take 'em some time. But we've got to get 'em well away from here or Garland may catch up some of these old packs to ride and then be able to rope the others."

Andy nodded wearily, "O.K. I'll hold the fort."

Wes got up and climbed stiffly on the palomino. "Stake out Sunny behind the rocks," he said, "but leave his saddle on. If you see Garland's men, line out and stay out of the way."

Whistling and swinging a rope's end, Wes drove the ponies over the edge of the butte and down a trail into the forest. Andy watched him go and suddenly felt very lonely.

He staked out Sunny close among the rocks. The feed wasn't very good, but here and there were clumps of bunch grass, and Sunny, hungry after his long gallop, made the most of them.

Big Joe Starts Closing In

Afraid to build a fire that might show Garland where their camp was, Andy ate some cold sausage and bread and butter, washed down with a can of tomato juice. When he had finished, he crawled up on a rock that faced west toward Lost Basin, and, watching great bands of yellow change to red, he forgot his troubles for a moment in the beauty of the sunset.

A cold wind was rising and, looking off to the east, he could see the clouds clearing away, lifting from the peaks and blowing in long garlands from the rimrock. There was no doubt about it; it was clearing up. To-morrow, at the latest, a plane could land in Lost Basin.

The sky began to fade, and Andy found himself listening. He could hear Sunny munching and tearing at the coarse grass and, way off somewhere, as darkness fell an owl awoke and began to hoot.

Andy shivered. The icy wind cut through his damp clothes. He wrapped himself in a blanket and lay like an Indian, a lonely figure, watching the distant ridge.

Suddenly his body stiffened. From down below he heard a yell. He looked toward the distant cabin and saw a light shining from its open door.

Who was it? Andy crawled over the rock for a better view. Excitement swept over him. "Sally!" he thought. "I'll bet it's Sally and the sheriff!" He was about to let out a whoop of welcome. The sound was starting from his lips, when he saw the flame.

It was small at first, a little flickering thing that might come from a campfire. But it began to grow. A column of smoke swirled out of the clearing, rose through the trees to the level of the butte, then blew away into wisps of nothingness.

Andy drew his breath in angrily. He saw the dry logs of the walls catch as the little cabin began to blaze up. The light cast flickering shadows against the wall of trees, and Andy could see figures running with blazing torches. Even the corral was burning now, and the men seemed to be piling things on the fire to make it roar higher. "Our pack panniers," Andy thought angrily, "our other bedroll, the tarps, everything. And the cabin isn't even ours!"

There was no reason for it. It was just revenge, Andy decided. A mean desire to destroy.

What would they do next? Andy thought he knew. He brought the two rifles up alongside him, and opened the extra boxes of ammunition. He was so angry that he forgot to be scared. "I'll have a reception ready," he thought, as he felt the cool barrel of his 30.30 against his cheek. He lined up the sights, wishing the little gun had the power to reach the fire. That would give 'em a scare.

He heard a sound behind him.

18

The Battle of the Butte

~~~~~~

*A*NDY SWUNG AROUND, HIS GUN AT THE READY. HE slipped off the safety catch and ran to the nearest rock behind him. There was a rustle in the bushes at the edge of the forest. Andy felt the panic in him. He raised the gun and was about to blaze into the trees when a voice said, "Powder River, Andy! Take it easy."

"Is that you, Uncle Wes?" Andy lowered the gun and his hands were shaking.

Uncle Wes rode out of the grove, pulled up the palomino, and dismounted gingerly onto a rock. "Looked like you might shoot me," he said. "What's the trouble?"

"Gee," Andy sat down weakly on the ground. "I almost did, Uncle Wes. Look on the other side. They're burning the cabin."

Uncle Wes leaned on a rock and gazed at the distant fire. For a long time he didn't speak, and Andy thought his face was strangely sad.

Finally he turned to Andy and said, "What a waste! It took a lot of work to build that cabin. Hand-hewn logs. Wooden pegs instead of nails. I spent a winter

212

trapping in here once. It was a nice, tight little place."

He roused himself, ate some food, then lit a cigarette. "Hit the hay, kid," he said. "We'll have to take turns standing watch."

Andy took the ax and redrove Sunny's stake so that he could reach fresh grass. He hoped that there were enough rocks around him, in case Garland or Big Joe tried a surprise attack.

He climbed into the bedroll. The clouds were almost gone now, and the sky was star-spattered. Andy felt the icy air blowing around the rock and plugged the hole with a food pannier. "It's clearing, Uncle Wes," he said. "That plane could get in by morning."

He heard his uncle pacing up and down restlessly, rubbing his hands to keep his fingers warm. Andy knew that there was something worrying him more than the plane, more than Big Joe, or even a possible attack. Where was Sally?

"Sally's O.K., Uncle Wes," he said aloud. "You know she can look after herself."

Wes's huge bulk loomed over him. Andy could just see the hatbrim cutting off a few stars. "Thanks, Andy," he said. "You're an understanding boy. Now get some sleep. You've got to stand watch before morning."

Andy thought he would never be able to sleep, but just the same a hand shaking the canvas tarp of the bedroll woke him up. He looked up to see that the stars were fading; the first gray edge of false dawn was lighting the horizon.

Andy crawled out of his warm nest. The air had a winter bite; there was white frost around the blankets where his breath had frozen.

"Aw, Uncle Wes," he said, shivering into his windbreaker. "You let me sleep all night."

"You needed it, boy." Uncle Wes looked grimy and tough, the gun sloping easily from his arm. "Now I'll catch a quick nap while you watch." He climbed into the bedroll. "If you hear or see anything, wake me up immediately, and don't let me sleep after sunrise." He was asleep almost before he had finished the sentence.

Andy slapped his arms around his body, starting the circulation, then went to inspect Sunny, who whinnied eagerly for breakfast.

Andy examined what he could see of the ground. Sunny had eaten everything within reach. But if he was moved he would no longer have the protection of the rocks. "Can't do it, old boy," he said. "You'll have to stick it out."

Sunny made a snuffling sound, fluttering his nostrils, and examined Andy for carrots. Andy took off the saddle and rubbed the back with the blanket. Sunny hadn't had a chance to roll since the long sweaty gallop of the day before, and was grateful for the wonderful scratching feeling along his spine. Andy resaddled, grabbed some dry bread, climbed, gun in hand, to the highest bit of rock, and gazed toward the cabin.

A pencil of smoke still rose from the ashes into the

growing dawn light. Andy hoped Big Joe had spent a cold night in the open.

With the glasses he examined the edges of the forest that surrounded the butte. There was nothing to see, not even a coyote or a bobcat. He gnawed on the bread and felt the icy breeze eat under his leather jacket.

He was staring gloomily at the smoke from the cabin, when from the corner of his eye something, some movement, caught his attention.

He turned quickly and looked directly below, where the timber ended and a clump of sagebrush obstructed the view. It might have been a jack rabbit or even a gopher, but Andy knew something had moved.

He sat quite still. The dawn was yellowing and things were becoming more distinct. Andy felt his breath coming fast, but he kept the glasses down.

There it was again, to the right of the highest bit of sage. Andy lifted the glasses, bringing the brush so close that he felt he could almost reach out and touch it.

There! He saw a blue sleeve, a hand, the dull metallic glint of a rifle barrel.

"Uncle Wes," he called, "they're here! They're coming." He didn't take his eyes off the brush, but he put down the glasses and picked up the gun. He heard Uncle Wes stir behind him. Then he felt a hand on his shoulder.

"Don't get trigger-happy, kid," Wes said, calmly. "Where did you see 'em?"

Andy pointed out the brush, and Wes had a look

215

through the glasses. For a long moment he watched, and Andy, feeling the tension rise within him, suddenly knew that this was the final day, the day of decision. This was the pay-off.

Either the plane came and took the enemy away, scot-free, or Sally and the sheriff arrived, or— Andy took a deep breath—or it was a fight to the finish on the top of this hill.

Wes put the glasses down, picked up the gun, and then, to Andy's surprise, turned and winked at him. "Hey, come out of that, Garland, or I'll bore a hole in you," he yelled.

Randy Garland rose from behind the sagebrush. "Hey, Marvin," he yelled. "I wanna talk to you."

"Then put down your gun and come up here," Wes said.

Andy saw Garland pass his gun backward into the brush. There were others, then, behind him. Andy looked at his uncle standing there with his eyes narrowed and just the hint of a smile around his bearded mouth. "Come on up and keep your hands out of your belt," Wes roared. He turned to Andy. "Look, kid," he said. "This may be a trick. I don't know what he wants, but while I talk to him, keep your eyes skinned. And shoot— get me?—shoot anyone who starts up that hill before Garland leaves."

"O.K., Uncle Wes." Andy tightened his belt and picked up his rifle.

"Remember"—Uncle Wes's voice was harsh—"no

matter what Garland and I do, keep your eyes on that timber."

Garland was crossing the open space now, his hands above his head, his eyes on Wes's rifle.

"Put down the gun, Marvin," he said, as he reached the rocks. "Nobody needs to get hurt."

"That's right," Wes answered, levelly. "But if anybody does, it's going to be you. Now what do you want?"

"I come to warn you, Wes," Garland said. "Big Joe sent me."

"I know that," Wes said. "You wouldn't have the nerve otherwise."

"Now lookit! All we want is to dangle out of here." Garland's voice was plaintive. Andy wished he dared look around and see his expression. But he kept his eyes on the rim of trees below, while he listened to the men behind him.

"Well, then, why don't you dangle? Who's stopping you?"

"That's what I come to explain. You got the horses somewheres. But we got a plane coming in today sure. You can't win nothin' by puttin' up a fight. Big Joe says that if you'll put down your guns and come along quiet, we'll let you loose as soon as the plane comes."

Andy heard his uncle laugh. "Bighearted Joe," he said. "Well, you tell him for me that the sheriff and a big posse will be in here this morning. They'll run you down one at a time, if they have to chase you from here to the Big Horns. And I'll make it my personal business to hog-tie Big Joe tighter'n a calf at a rodeo."

"That's big talk, bub." Garland's voice began to get mean. "Big Joe's tryin' to be nice to an old broke-down .ieel. He's got a dozen men out there. They got tommy-guns. They're killers back home, racketeers-like. They'll fill you so full 'er lead you'll—"

Andy didn't hear the rest of the sentence because of Sunny's snort of fear. He swung around and saw the little horse backing to the end of the picket rope attached to his ankle. His ears were back; his teeth showed. Below him there was movement. A rifle slid through the cover. A man made a running dive for a boulder partway up the side of the hill.

"Uncle Wes, they're coming! They're after our horses," Andy yelled. He raised his carbine and jerked the trigger. That guy was after Sunny. Sunny'd given the alarm. Anger swelled up in him. The bullet spat too far to the left, and the man ducked behind a rock.

Andy fired again, but he was so angry he couldn't see what he was doing. To kill a horse! To creep up and try to kill Sunny! He fired a third time, chipping a piece of rock from above the man's head, forcing him to make a desperate dive back into the brush.

Andy could see others now, creeping here and there in the timber, surrounding them. He wished Uncle Wes would join him. He could never keep them off by himself.

Then he heard Wes say, "Why, you double-crossing rat. You're just stalling." There was the hard clumping sound of a fist against flesh, and Andy darted a quick look behind him. He saw Garland stagger into a rock, blood flowing from his lip. He saw Wes charge him, his fists working like locomotive pistons crashing into the other's body, feeling for a vital spot.

Then Garland kicked at Wes's bad ankle. He leaped from the rock, stamping at Wes's foot, trying to make him lose balance.

At the same moment, there was a smack of lead against rock, followed by the harsh spitting of a tommy-gun from below. Andy spun around. Big Joe's men were opening up, bullets whined, ricocheting with thin screams. Rifles cracked, and Andy, his hands clammy with sweat, slid his gun over the boulder in front of him.

It was blind, wild, uphill shooting, Andy thought. He saw that Big Joe's men were keeping well under cover, trying to blast terror into him and his uncle.

He strained his eyes, trying to find someone to fire at. Behind him, he heard the two men tearing at each other. Fists thudded against flesh. There were great sobbing breaths.

He dared not look around again. He lined up the sights of his rifle, waiting for the attack.

Then a great thumping sound, the fall of two straining bodies, came to him. They were down! Garland was heavier. Garland was winning. He had to turn, take his eyes away from the timber for a second.

He swung around, his rifle ready.

219

The two men were behind a boulder. He could still hear them driving at each other's throats.

Behind them, Andy could see Sunny straining at his stake, his eyes white with terror, his forefeet pulled taut in front of him as he tried to pull the stake out by the roots.

Then the sounds from Wes and Garland stopped.

Andy wanted to rush behind the rock and see what had happened. He half turned to run, but as he did so he heard yells from the forest. He thought the advance was on, and he remembered his uncle's orders. "Keep your eyes on the timber."

He turned and fired at the figures flitting from tree to tree. He could hear shouts behind him. They were encircled now for sure, and there was no chance to stop them if they advanced all at once. He reloaded grimly.

Then the tommygun, which had been the signal to open fire, ceased, and the other guns stopped with it.

Big Joe shouted, "Come on out, Marvin, or I'll come and get you!"

Andy turned and looked at the rock where he had last heard the two men fighting, but he didn't hear Wes answer.

The sudden stillness was ominous, heavy. Was Uncle Wes—?

He saw a foot move. Someone was breathing hard.

Andy raised his rifle and waited. He let the bead fall into the groove of the rear sight. If it was Garland, if

Garland came out from behind that rock alone, Andy knew what he must do.

A hand showed around the corner. Then an arm. Uncle Wes, holding to the rock, slid into view.

Andy let the rifle down with a sigh. "Uncle Wes! What happened?" he croaked.

"Garland's taking a little nap," Wes said. "The no-good-bear-bait tried to stomp on my bum ankle."

Wes grinned almost happily, Andy thought, and wiped his face with his sleeve. "Give me that rifle, boy," he said cheerfully, "and don't look so sad. This isn't Custer's last stand."

Andy grinned back ruefully and passed Uncle Wes his gun. "Can I shinny out there and free Sunny?" he asked.

Before Wes could answer, the matter was decided by the rattle of the tommygun. This was followed by another fusilade of pistols and rifles of various calibers.

Andy ducked, but Wes calmly slid up on the rock beside him, his rifle at his side. "You go back and cover Sunny," he said. "Don't fire until they show themselves. That's the silliest, wildest shootin' I've ever seen." Andy slid back to the rock that covered Sunny and tried to talk to him over the sound of the guns. Bullets whistled in all directions, but mostly high. Big Joe and his boys weren't used to long-range firing, Andy thought gleefully. They might plug somebody in a back alley of a city, but they'd never knocked over a mountain sheep at six hundred yards, like his Uncle Wes.

He looked back. Uncle Wes was lying there on his rock, seemingly quite relaxed. In fact, he was rolling a smoke.

Then, quite suddenly, the advance started. Men crawled from the timber and, taking advantage of every bush, started snaking their way toward the rocks.

Andy started firing, but Sunny's squeals worried him so that he felt sure he never hit anyone. Wes, lying on his boulder, coolly picked out his target. Mechanically, his hand slipped back the lever; his finger squeezed the trigger. He fired at legs, because he wanted these men to live to face a jury.

His accuracy was deadly. Each time one of Big Joe's men dashed forward, Wes's rifle cracked and the man went down. His comrades saw him clutching his leg. They heard his yell of pain and they hugged the earth, shooting wildly at the rocks above.

A ricochet hit Sunny in the rump. Screaming and pulling back with all his might, he yanked the stake out by the roots and galloped in behind the rocks.

The firing grew more erratic and gradually died down, until only an occasional shot sang over Andy's head. He jumped down and ran to Sunny, who was quivering behind a boulder. He wouldn't let Andy touch the wound. His rump swung away and his head waved wildly.

Andy heard his uncle's voice behind him. "It's all right, kid," he said. "Only creased him. A little salve to keep off the flies and he'll be O.K."

The firing ceased entirely, and Big Joe's boys retreated to the protection of the woods. Now that it was over for the moment, Andy felt weak in the knees. He slumped down to the ground.

His uncle, one eye on the forest below, brought him a canteen of water. "Take it easy, boy," he said. "I'll call you if I need you."

19
Return of the DC-3

~~~~~~

*T*HE SUN WAS HIGH NOW, AND IT BEAT DOWN CRUELLY. From under a rock, Garland, tied hand and foot, groaned fitfully.

Wes had the glasses to his eyes. He was looking toward the divide, at the distant, bare slopes where a pack train would show up. Where was Sally? Had she been intercepted by Big Joe?

Down below, Andy could hear the men talking in the woods. He wondered if they were planning another attack, whether Big Joe was threatening them, forcing them into the open to face Wes's deadly carbine. He tried to catch some of their words, but what he heard was the sound of a plane.

He looked toward the east, and over the distant rims came the old DC-3 headed straight for the Garland camp in Lost Basin.

There were wild yells from below, ragged cheers, and a great crashing of bodies going through underbrush.

Uncle Wes crawled off his rock and put down his gun. He suddenly looked older, Andy thought. The light

Over the distant rims came the old DC-3, headed straight for the Garland camp in Lost Basin.

of battle had gone from his eyes. He had done his best, and it looked now as though he had lost.

"Shall we follow 'em, Uncle Wes?" Andy asked wearily.

"Plenty of time," Wes grunted. "If they take along the boys I shot in the legs, it'll be three hours before they can get to the landing field. We'll go down and have a look at the trail to the divide. I just can't figger about Sally and the sheriff."

Andy went back to Sunny, who had calmed somewhat, and patted the little horse until he was able to have a good look at the wound. The bullet had just crossed the top of the rump, tearing the skin but hardly cutting the flesh.

At his uncle's suggestion, he cut a piece of fat from the haunch of bacon in the pack panniers and rubbed the grease all around the wound to protect it from flies.

Uncle Wes, hobbling more than ever from the kick on his ankle, shoved the moaning Garland under the shadow of a rock. "You've got lots of time, Randy," he said, "to think what a jury of good cowmen are going to do to you." Then he took the glasses and looked over the country.

Andy watched him from the shade of a boulder. "See anything?" he asked.

"Nothing but those pack rats climbing up the Lost Basin trail," Wes answered. "Let's go."

They climbed on their horses and started down the

226

hill. There was no movement in the timber. Evidently nobody wanted to stay as a rear guard.

When they reached the ruins of the little cabin, Wes rode up the trail for several miles toward the divide looking for tracks, while Andy tried to salvage what he could of their belongings.

Wes came back, shaking his head. "No sign of the sheriff," he said, gloomily. "Let's watch the take-off. Maybe they'll have trouble getting off that muddy field."

Cautiously they worked their way up the Lost Basin trail, following the footsteps of the retreating dudes.

"Maybe we could find some way to bang up that plane," Andy said, without conviction. "Could you hit the gas tanks in the wings?"

"Doubt it." Wes shook his head sadly. "Too long a shot from the ridge, and those fellows would make mince-meat of us if we got close."

Near the top of the ridge, they dismounted and led their horses off the trail. Climbing through the undergrowth, rifles ready, they worked their way to the crest.

They could hear the yelling as they reached the top. Peering over the edge at a point where the cliff was steep on the further side, they saw the motley crew crossing the meadow. Some were limping and two of them were being carried. The last two men, and one of them Andy felt sure was Big Joe, covered the retreat. Andy could see the short nozzle of the tommygun pointed in their direction.

The plane had landed, taxied to the end of the field,

and turned for the take-off. Andy noticed that it had made no tracks in the meadow. The hot sun had already dried the turf. There was no hope there. He looked at his uncle.

Wes's face was a mask. He showed no signs of the anger or the hopelessness he felt at losing the fight. A mountain man rarely shows sorrow or pain, Andy thought. But Wes's eyes were following Big Joe as he retreated across the meadow.

The men clambered in, hurriedly. They had no desire to fight now, to meet the sheriff they knew was coming. Their camp was left standing, the tent flaps fluttering in the breeze.

Big Joe got aboard the plane last, his gun still at the ready. The door closed.

The motors warmed up separately. First the right one roared, then the left. They sounded in sweet condition. At last the plane quivered and began to move.

If only it would hit a stump, a boulder, anything, Andy thought, as the silver ship gathered headway. But it roared on, leaving the ground gracefully in plenty of time to clear the forest.

Andy got up and shook his fist as the plane tore over them. But Wes just sat on a rock, looking at the camp below.

Andy didn't know how long they sat there. Now that it was all over and they had lost the fight, he felt a terrible fatigue creep over him. He didn't care if he never moved again.

228

Return of the DC-3

He looked at the little horse grazing near him. Even Sunny seemed to have lost his pep. He'd grown thinner in the last few days. For the first time since Andy had owned him, his ribs showed. Dried sweat caked around his neck and eyes. Well, he'd done his best, too, Andy thought. In fact he'd done more than anybody.

"Come on. Let's go," said Wes, helping himself off the rock with his gun. "We've got a lot of work to do."

"Gee." Andy stood up wearily. "What now, Uncle Wes? I thought it was all over."

Wes turned on him suddenly, almost angrily. "All over, my eye!" he growled.

"Well, what can we do now?"

"I've got the plane license number. I have information on their hunting licenses. We've got the evidence of their camp. And best of all we've got that yellow pup, Garland. I'm going after 'em till I find 'em. Then I'm going to have them extradited to face trial in this state if it takes me the rest of my life."

Andy looked at his uncle in wonder. Wes looked as determined as ever. "O.K., boss," Andy tried to grin. "What do we do first?"

They rode down to the Garland camp and found it a shambles. Panniers were strewn everywhere. Unburied garbage had been dumped over the edge of the knoll into the creek bottom, and flies had collected from miles around. They bit Andy on his sweaty neck and face and he wished his uncle would leave, but Wes was making inventory of everything. Finally, he looked up

229

and saw Andy standing around, slapping fitfully at the darting deerflies.

"I tell you what you do," he said kindly. "Ride up to the upper end of the basin and see if you can find our horses. We're going to need 'em too—"

He stopped suddenly and listened. Andy heard it, too. A plane! Were they coming back for something? Had they decided to return for Garland?

It came over the ridge, low and fast.

"Duck behind that sagebrush," Wes snapped, "and have your gun ready. If they come in that means they've decided to fight for Garland. He must know too much."

20

Sally Packs a Gun

~~~~~~~~~~~~~~~~~~~~~~~~~~~~~~~~~~~~

ANDY COULD FEEL THE WIND STIR THE HAIR ON THE back of his neck. It was blowing up the basin. That meant they would land, coming into the wind, right near camp.

He slid close to his clump of sage and heard Wes, off to his right, cock his rifle. There would be no shooting at the legs this time. They were out in the open, sitting ducks unless they shot to kill.

Andy saw the plane hit the earth easily, bump a couple of times on the uneven slopes, and start taxiing directly toward the camp.

Big Joe must have seen them from the plane. There was no hiding, even if Sunny and the palomino weren't in open view at the corrals. For a moment, Andy wished fervently that they had taken the horses and made a run for it.

He looked at his uncle, and Wes smiled at him, with the light of battle once again in his eyes. Andy didn't envy the first man to jump from that plane.

He saw Wes beginning to crawl forward toward a

gnarled tree. A better place from which to cover the door, Andy thought.

The plane roared toward the knoll, turned so that the door faced them—and the barrel of Wes's rifle.

"Don't shoot until I say so," Wes said, his cheek close to the side of his gun.

"O.K." Andy raised his little carbine, settled the bead in the groove of the rear sight, and aimed at the door.

But for some reason the target seemed to waver, either from waves of heat between him and the plane or because he was rattled. He felt his heart pounding at the ground. His trigger finger was sweaty and ice-cold, and he felt his left hand holding the gun shake.

The door opened slowly. It was high off the ground and the man who opened it had to lower himself gingerly.

It was Big Joe.

Andy felt the sweat in his eyes. He could hardly see the figure. His muscles tensed; his trigger finger started to squeeze.

But Uncle Wes didn't say anything.

Another man dropped from the plane, then another and another. Andy felt himself choking. He wanted to cry out. What was Uncle Wes thinking of? They'd be outnumbered, overwhelmed.

Then suddenly it struck him. He lowered the rifle, wiped his eyes with his sleeve to clear them, and looked again at the motley crowd jumping from the door. There wasn't a gun among them and—and their hands were up.

Sally Packs a Gun

As the last man made the jump, a slim, boyish figure with wild blond hair appeared in the entrance holding in her hand a large Colt .45.

"Sally!" Andy was on his feet in a second, but even then Wes was ahead of him.

Sally jumped to the ground, and behind her appeared the sheriff with another revolver, his mustachios twirled upward in a widening grin.

"Hey, you cowboys," he shouted. "Seems like to me we're one varmint short. Where's Garland?"

"We've got him," Wes yelled, before grabbing Sally in his arms.

Suddenly, Andy felt terribly dirty. He looked down at his stained Californias, his dirty shirt full of dried mud and brambles. One hand crept up to his sweaty face, the other through his tangled hair.

Sally was running toward him, looking trim in her faded jeans and her white silk shirt with the yellow bandanna around her neck.

She ran up to him, threw her arms around his dirty neck, and hugged him. "Andy," she cried. "Andy, you wonderful, dirty old bum, you! You look like a real mountain man at last!"

"Powder River!" Andy said weakly, and began to laugh.

The plane, with two deputies aboard, left with the prisoners, and that night after a dinner that made Andy feel visibly swollen, they built a roaring campfire. The flames crackled into the starlit night. Horses whinnied to each other across the meadow. While Wes and the sheriff smoked, Sally told her part of the story.

"First of all I got hold of the sheriff," she said. "He telephoned Dad's deputies and sent two of 'em with pack horses up the trail, while we traced the plane."

"Andy and I could have used a couple of deputies this morning," said Wes wryly. "Where were they?"

"Stuck behind a washout on Bear Creek," the sheriff said. "Heard about it this morning. A cloudburst blowed the trail into the creek for a hundred yards. Ranger's got a crew on it right now."

Sally told how, with the help of the airline men, they had traced the plane to Miles City, Montana, where it stopped to refuel. When it returned, they were waiting for it and had the owners arrested. Then, with their own pilot, they flew in to Lost Basin.

"It was the doggonedest thing I ever see!" The sheriff shook his head. "Here was this bunch of low-life hombres with enough guns to attack a fort stumblin' and helpin' each other across the meaders. An' here was you an' Andy asittin' on the ridge lookin' like you dasn't chase 'em."

"We do all right at long range," Wes said, smiling. "But if we'd gone on that meadow, we'd have been blown to pieces."

"That's what the sheriff said," Sally took up the story. "So we all crammed into the pilot's compartment, locked the door, and came in for a landing. Those men climbed in like they were chased by a million grizzlies. They hollered at us to get going and we said 'sure' and took off. Then, when they were all settled down congratulating each other, we opened the door and got the drop on them. Gee, they sure were surprised."

The talk went on far into the night. Gradually the fire died down, but Andy, toasting his feet by the coals, listened, and his ears burned at the things his uncle and Sally said about him.

Finally, the sheriff got up, stretched and said, "Well, seems like to me we ain't givin' full credit where it's due at that. How about that little old sorrel horse? He sure done his share. He run off the Garland cavvy. He brought Andy out to the ranger station. He warned Andy when that attack started this morning. Don't give the boy so much credit, Wes, and give the horse a little more."

"I don't know," Sally said sleepily. "Sunny's just about the best horse I ever saw, but gee, it was Andy gentled him."

21

Sunny Receives a Reward

~~~~~~~~~~~~~~~~~~~~~~~~~~~~~~~~~~~

*D*OWN IN THE VALLEY OF THE SOUTH FORK THE roundup was over and the cattle shipped. The new snow powdered the lower rimrocks, and the coyotes howled their warning of the coming winter. The deer came down off the sidehills and began to get into the rancher's haystacks. Hunters appeared from the hills with their meat, and old Sam, the trapper, wrangled in his pack string, oiled his traps, and prepared to leave for the deep woods.

It was time for Andy to go home. Telegrams from his father, telling him that school had opened, wouldn't allow him to put it off any longer.

Old Jack Walther who drove the mail stage was due early that day. There wasn't much time to say good-by. When his last bags were packed, Andy finally slipped away from his Aunt Ida and ran down to the corral.

He felt strange in his Eastern clothes. The low shoes with thin soles seemed terribly fragile. He'd grown so much that his trousers were too short, and the collar of his shirt nearly choked him. His hat, after wearing a

Stetson, seemed ridiculously small. What would Sunny think when he saw his master in dude clothes?

He entered the corral and called softly, "Sunny! Oats! Carrots!"

Up snapped the little head from the hayrack. The ears pricked forward, the nostrils fluttered a soft greeting. "What's happened to the boss?" he seemed to say. "Those are sure strange duds." Sunny walked up to Andy, his head out. "But it *is* the boss. I know that voice. I know those carrots."

Andy couldn't speak again. He held out his hand and felt the soft, mushy nose he loved so much with the little prickly whiskers and the underlip that searched for food. He scrubbed the soft golden hair around the ears.

He choked a little and turned away. He could hear the pony following, but he didn't look back. He hurried through the gate toward the house and ran blindly into Sally.

"Andy." Sally stopped him. "I know how you feel," she said quickly. "I gotta leave Pint and go to High School in town. But I'll be back week ends and I'll make sure Sunny's all right. I'll feed him carrots and stuff. I just wanted you to know he'd be cared for."

"By golly," Andy thought. "She sure understands." He yelled after the retreating figure the highest compliment he could think of. "Ride him, Sally!" he yelled. "You ride him all you like."

The stage came and Old Jack was in a hurry. He

had a lot of pickups to make and a side trip into a dude ranch down river. He hustled Andy into the truck. Uncle Wes patted Andy on the shoulder and invited him out the following year. Aunt Ida cried, but Sally was nowhere to be seen.

Old Jack threw the car into gear and was just about to start when a great rattling sound interrupted him. Around the corner, steaming and bubbling like an old kettle, came the sheriff's car with the old man stiff and straight behind the wheel.

"Pull up there, Jack," he called, grinding his jalopy to a stop.

"Can't wait," said Jack.

"You wait in the name of the law," the sheriff said cheerfully, "or I'll put a slug in your tires. I got official business with Andy Marvin."

He yanked a box from the back seat and walked over to them. From his pocket he drew forth an official-looking envelope. He handed it to Andy.

"Letter from the Governor," he said. "An' this here box is from him, too."

Puzzled, Andy opened the letter. Under the state seal he read:

DEAR ANDY MARVIN:
Sheriff Tex Blackwell has brought to my attention the fine services you have rendered the state and your country by working with your uncle to protect the game in the Big Game Creek Country.

Sunny Receives a Reward

If we are going to keep our game and our hunting for the benefit of our citizens, we need people like you to help us to do it. Otherwise, elk, antelope, Big Horn sheep, and other Rocky Mountain game will disappear like the buffalo.

In behalf of the State Game Commission and the citizens of the state, I should like to express my appreciation to you and your uncle. You have done a fine service in bringing these game poachers to justice. I hope the sentence of the courts will be a warning to all others who have the inclination to kill wantonly the wildlife of our country.

I understand that a certain sorrel horse named Sunny was of considerable help in tracking and pursuing the lawbreakers, and I take pleasure in sending you something for the horse and yourself as a slight token of my appreciation.

Sincerely—

The Governor's signature was scrawled across the bottom.

Andy opened the box. In it was the most beautiful bridle of hand-tooled leather that he had ever seen. Silver conchos engraved with his initials decorated the headstall, and a short, Wyoming-type, curb bit inlaid with silver and copper looked just right for Sunny's mouth.

Andy couldn't speak. He looked for Sally. He wanted to give her the bridle and ask her to try it on Sunny, but she was nowhere to be seen.

Andy thanked the sheriff as best he could and hugged Aunt Ida and Uncle Wes once again.

Old Jack ripped into gear, and they rumbled through the ranch gate.

The road made a turn around a high butte after it left the Marvin ranch. Andy didn't look up for a while. He didn't want Old Jack to see his face.

"Looks like she's agoin' to blow." Old Jack pointed to thin wisps of frost cloud sliding up the canyons from the east, slicing along the rimrock, bringing winter to the valley.

"Yeah," Andy said and looked up at the butte. They were standing on the crest, a slim girl with wild blond hair that almost matched the gold of the horse's mane. That's why she had disappeared! She wanted him to see his horse just once more, to have a last picture to take back with him of Sunny against the mountains.

Andy waved back wildly to show he understood.

He wished he could hear Sunny nicker. The car rounded a hill, but when next he saw the butte, the girl and the horse were still there.

"Comin' back next summer?" Old Jack asked, trying to make conversation.

Andy swallowed the lump in his throat. His eyes were still on the distant butte.

"You're doggone right," he said gruffly. "I sure am!"

240

www.ingramcontent.com/pod-product-compliance
Lightning Source LLC
Chambersburg PA
CBHW020803250626
47155CB00003B/1184